Prologue

"I'm telling you. I saw another side of him when they kidnapped Dianna last year." Michael St. John, Sr. drives his golf cart while talking to his best friend and partner in crime, Matthew Phillips, Sr.

"Do you think he's ready to settle down and be with one woman?"

Mike Sr. stops in front of the golf course hole they are going to play on. "I think he is. He just doesn't know it yet."

Matt Sr. gets out of the cart to grab his golf clubs. "Your son Michael is buck wild. I think he is worse than James was before he married Dianna. He does not seem to have a caring bone in his body, especially when it comes to settling down with one woman."

"Yeah, I thought the same thing until I watched him last year with Tamara, Dianna's best friend from New York. Remember when we were looking for Dianna and Tamara joined us out in L.A? He showed a sensitive side I had never seen before. I have never seen him take care of any woman the way he took care of her."

"You think she's the one?"

"No. Their relationship is platonic. He finally broke it down

1

to me. They are just friends and when everything happened, they truly were just supporting each other during the crisis. He said when she came to Memphis for the wedding and stayed with him at his condo, they did not sleep together and never have."

Matt Sr. makes his putt. "Well, that answers that. They really must be simply good friends if they have stayed in the same house together and never slept with each other."

"I know. They make such a cute couple but if it is not there, as good as we are with getting people together, we cannot make something happen if there are no sparks between them. I think they both are big players and just like to flirt with each other. I also think they get a kick out of confusing people about their relationship."

"Now that sounds like something your crazy son would enjoy doing, and you know if Tamara is Dianna's friend, she is just as crazy as Dianna. I can see how they are close friends and just like messing with people about their friendship, but it doesn't solve the problem of us finding him someone to settle down with."

Mike Sr. and Matt Sr. have been best friends for over fifty years and were previous law partners at the civil law firm they owned. They both are in their sixties and, like their sons, are over six feet tall. Mike Sr. is a caramel skin color with black curly hair that is slightly gray with dimples, and Matt Sr. is dark-skinned with salt and pepper hair. Both are slim and trim from playing golf all day since they have retired. After retirement, they left their law firm to Michael and his law partner, Bruce Newman, to run. As matchmakers, they got their two kids, Matthew and Christina, together and their other golf buddy, Charlie Thomas's son, James with Christina's best friend, Dianna Wright, last year.

Both men, along with Charlie, are grandfathers and you would think they would be content, but now they want to get Mike Sr.'s only son, Michael, married. They feel now that all their children are married except him, so he should be next.

"I think it's time we stop by our law firm to see if there is anyone there who might catch our eye that he could settle down with." Mike Sr. smiles because he loves a new adventure, and he knows to get his son to settle down is going to be quite the adventure.

"This will be the hardest one to date. Michael truly has no interest in just one woman. You would think since his two best friends are married and fathers, he would at least slow down a bit."

Mike Sr. gets back into the golf cart to drive to the next hole. "That's why it's time for us to step in and find him a woman. The first step is to get him to just date one woman at a time and then we will pull out the big guns to get married."

Matt Sr. smiles and gets into the other side of the cart. "That sounds like a plan to me. Let the games begin."

Chapter One

"Girl, you're crazy as hell." Michael St. John II laughs while talking to his buddy, Tamara Walker, as he cleans off his desk to go into a meeting. He glances out his office window at the weather that is still nice. Even though it is September, it is usually not cold in Memphis, TN.

"I'm telling you, Michael." Tamara's wide eyes stare into space. "Why would I want to settle down with this man when I know how pilots are? I work with them every day. Just because he flies for Delta Airlines and I work for American Airlines, what makes him think I do not know how some pilots are with messing around with different flight attendants? I live the same way he does. I was just fine hooking up with him when we both are in the same city, but no, he wants to have a relationship."

Michael shakes his head and cracks up laughing. "I told you about hooking up with all those jerks you keep picking up." He stands up to put on the jacket to his suit before he looks over the file to discuss in his meeting. "You know you're supposed to be my baby mama. See, we wouldn't be having all these problems with you messing around with all these different men. We would have our beautiful baby who would stay with you for six months in New York and then stay with me here in Memphis for six months and that way, neither of us would have time to play around with other people. We would have the best of both worlds. Come on in," he hollers out to Randall Johnson, one of his senior attorneys and running buddy in Memphis.

"I know that's right." Tamara takes off her flight clothes to get into the shower. "I think I'll go out tonight to meet me some fresh new men."

"Okay baby, just don't pick up anyone like those last two. I thought we would never get rid of them. I almost had to kick their asses to get them out of the picture."

"I know you're not talking when you had a stalker. I told you that girl was going to be trouble, but you wouldn't listen."

"Yeah, but she was so good in the bed."

Tamara laughs. "That's going to be the death of you yet, a good piece of ass."

"Well, at least I get something out of it when all you get is drama. I was thinking about coming to New York to see you, are you going to be there?"

"I think so, darling. I'll check my schedule and I'll call you back to let you know."

"Okay, the love of my life. I have a three o'clock meeting I'm getting ready to go into. I'll talk to you when I talk to you."

"Okay, sweetheart... have a good day. Talk to you when I talk to you."

They always say goodbye to each other with the same line because they never know when they will talk to each other again. From day one, they ended all their the same way, conversations whether face-to-face or over the phone. Good friends with each other who flirt and talk to each other in a special way that most people not only thought they were a couple but also married, their relationship confuses everyone in their families because neither wants to settle down. They say they are only best friends, but their interactions with each other show something else.

"What?" Michael half-smiles and asks Randall, who stands there shaking his head.

"Man, I don't get your relationship with Tamara. She is fine as hell and you two keep up with each other as if you're married. You all in her business and she's all into yours, but you have never dated or even slept together."

"I know." Michael grins, shows his famous dimples, straightens his red silk tie, and picks up the file to take into the meeting. "We just have a special relationship. We bonded when they kidnapped Dianna last year and have remained close ever since. Best friends, even though no one wants to believe that because she's a woman and I'm a man. Everyone feels we can't only be friends, but we are. That line has not been crossed and we do not plan to cross it. Once we cross the line of friendship, that's when all the drama starts and neither of us want drama, so we'll just remain close friends."

"Something ain't right. It's just not normal for a man and woman to be so close and not have messed around with each other. Since you have not had that and do not want it, why don't you hook me up with her?"

"Hell no." Michael frowns and raises his voice at his friend. "I will not hook you up with my best friend. I know you are no good."

Randall laughs at him, pointing his finger in his face. "See what I mean? You do not want to share her with anyone, but you claim you do not want her for yourself. I'm telling you, you two have a sick relationship."

Michael ignores Randall to stop by Lisa's office to let her know he is going into his meeting, but if Tamara calls to get him because he is waiting for her to call back with some information.

Lisa O'Neal and Randall look at each other because, like everyone else, she does not understand their relationship either. She has been Michael's personal assistant for five years who takes care of his business and personal schedule. Lisa is five-four with mocha-colored skin, slanted dark brown eyes, and is a divorced mother of two little boys. She had never heard of Tamara until last year after he came back from L.A. where he had a family emergency. Now, she knows Tamara is a top priority and when she calls, he always takes her calls. They even travel together, but he still has all his other women he plays around with.

"Michael, do you need me to send some flowers to Tanya, your date you stood up last night?" Lisa looks up, still on top of things about his personal life.

"I forgot all about her. No, don't send any flowers because she will think I still want to see her when I'm over that." Michael sighs as he heads down the long hall to go to the conference room.

St. John, Phillips, and Newman, Attorneys at Law is the law firm his dad and his Uncle Matt opened before he got out of high school. He went to Harvard Law with James and Matthew, his two best friends who he has known all his life. Matthew, now married to his sister, Christina who has made him an uncle to one-year-old, Zachary Nigel Phillips. James, Michael's former partying buddy, married Dianna and they have a one-year-old daughter, Kennedy Dianna Thomas, who he views as a play niece as well. They all live in L.A. while Michael still lives in Memphis.

The law firm specializes in civil law and has offices on the entire eighth floor in the Renaissance Center, along the prestigious Poplar Avenue Corridor on Aaron Brenner Drive. Michael lives downtown in a condo on the bluff in The Shrine Building Condominiums because that is where all the action is if you live in Memphis. All the young urban people live and party in downtown Memphis where any night of the week, you can hangout on Beale Street or eat at one of the many restaurants. Michael mainly works in Memphis but is always traveling to L.A. to see family. He goes to New York to hang out with Tamara and Florida to just hangout. He loves Miami, Orlando, and has a house in Key West. The house in Key West is where he goes to chill and regroup from work and partying. He has never shared his house in Key West with any family member or woman.

Waiting for him in the conference room are fifteen of the twenty-five attorneys who work there along with Bruce Newman, who is a partner. There are three senior attorneys and they are getting ready to hire the fourth one from Atlanta, Ga. This is what some of the meeting is going to be about: to discuss the new attorney they are going to hire to join the firm.

"What's up everybody, let's get down to business." Michael sits at the head of the conference table. Laid back and known with family and friends to be a complete nut, Michael is serious in business and a shark who does not play in the courtroom.

"Let us discuss bringing on this new attorney and then we can go over the caseload. I want everyone's input on whether you feel we need to add another senior attorney. Bruce has been interviewing Amber Anderson from Atlanta, GA. I have not met her, so I'm going to let Bruce tell us about her, so we can discuss."

Bruce Newman is five eleven with dark brown skin color and a low haircut. Quiet and reserved, he wears eyeglasses and is a practicing attorney along with handling the firm's business affairs. Clearing his throat, Bruce chimes in. "Amber Anderson has been a DA in Fulton county in Georgia for five years and has not lost one case. She is a hard worker, very devoted to her career, and comes highly recommended by her law professors and several prominent attorneys in Atlanta."

Right before they get ready to discuss the new attorney, Lisa interrupts Michael with a phone call from Tamara.

"Hey baby, what's the deal? Are you going to be in New York for a while?"

"I'll be here all next week until I leave out next Sunday afternoon heading to L.A. before I must go to Europe, so if you're coming, you need to get here Friday. That way baby, we can hang out all weekend and next week."

"Why don't I come Friday evening after work and then we hang out there in New York until Thursday? Do you want to go out to L.A. to see the kids? We can do some serious partying and that way, you'll already be out there in L.A. to fly out straight to Europe."

"Okay, let me get us a flight out of here for Thursday. Do you want to fly out morning or evening?"

"Let's get a flight out in the afternoon. Do you think we can catch some of the US Open tennis match before we leave for L.A.?"

"I'm sure we can. I'll call my brother, Joshua, for his box seats for one day at the tennis match and book us a flight out for Thursday afternoon. I'll talk to you when I talk to you."

"Alright baby, talk to you when I talk to you."

Michael turns around after talking to Tamara on the conference room phone to continue his meeting. "Okay, tell me some more about Ms. Amber Anderson and why we should bring her on as a senior attorney, besides never losing a case and good recommendations. I need to know if she will fit in at this office, but also why she wants to do civil law when she's been in the DA's office since law school."

"She wants to do civil law because the DA's office has interfered with her personal life, and she's ready to practice a different type of law. She also stated she is ready to get out of Atlanta to start fresh." Bruce passes Amber's file to Michael to review.

"Well...she needs to be ready to work hard because some of our cases can be difficult. I hope she's ready to devote herself. What I will do is review her file while I'm flying to New York on Friday. I will know more about her after reading her file, but I trust your judgment Bruce, so we probably have a new senior attorney." Michael sets her file aside to continue the meeting.

Chapter Two

W hile reading Amber's file on his flight to New York Friday evening, Michael learns she is a prosecuting attorney from Atlanta, GA who has not lost a case, as Bruce stated. She graduated summa cum laude from University of Georgia and magna cum laude from Harvard Law School. Michael knows from reading her file she probably is a nerd and a workaholic. That is fine with him; he just wants someone who can handle a heavy caseload and will work hard. Bruce has done all the interviewing so far and will be the one to hire her. He will meet her when he gets back from New York and L.A.

He puts her file back into his briefcase as the plane prepares to land. Michael walks through JFK where women are turning their heads, watching him as he goes to meet Tamara. Dressed in a navy-blue suit standing at six-two, the thirty-five-year-old has a pecan skin color, light brown eyes with long eyelashes, black wavy hair which is cut short, a moustache and goatee, and some of the cutest dimples you will ever see. He always turns heads wherever he goes. Once he steps out the door in front of American Airlines, there stands his buddy, Tamara, waiting for him. She is beautiful and every time Michael sees her, the thirty-three-year-old is more gorgeous than ever. She is standing there with her hands on her hips, telling some man off to get out of her face. Tamara always has men hitting on her wherever she is. Men love Tamara, and Tamara loves men. No wonder he is trying to talk to her with a short dress on, fitting like a glove. She stands at five-nine with olive skin color, hazel eyes, long eyelashes, a straight nose, and naturally curly black hair that hangs down her back.

Michael walks over to where she is standing. "Hey baby...have you been waiting long?"

Tamara stops telling the man off when she sees him standing there. "Sweetheart, I'm so glad you're here. Will you please tell this man we have been married for ten years and just because I don't have my wedding ring on because I lost it does not mean I do not have a husband?"

"I'm sorry, my man, but she is not single. My wife has lost three wedding rings in the last ten years."

The man stammers. "I'm sorry, man. I didn't mean to hit on your wife, please forgive me."

Michael places his hand on Tamara's waist to lead her to the car. "That's okay. I know she is beautiful, that's the reason I married her for her beauty and her cooking."

Tamara and Michael walk to her car, cracking up laughing. They love to mess with people, especially since everyone always assumes they are married when they are together.

"Where the hell did you get that from about my cooking? You know I don't cook."

"Just like you know we have not been married for ten years, but I like the losing of the ring thing; that's a new one." Michael puts his luggage in her trunk then opens the door for her to sit on the passenger side of her car because he always drives her Jaguar when they are together since they have the same cars. His is a black XK8 convertible and hers is a gray XK8 convertible as well.

"I know. That is my new thing when guys approach me and I do not want to be bothered. I tell them I am married. I just thought of the ring thing when some guy said to me you don't have on a wedding ring, so now I tell everyone I lost it."

Michael throws his head back and laughs. Tamara and Dianna

are the only two women he knows who have a wicked sense of humor. He drives through Manhattan like he lives there on the Upper East Side for them to go get something to eat. They go to the Russian Tea Room to have dinner. This is both of their favorite restaurant and as usual, when they walk in somewhere together, all heads turn because they are a beautiful couple, even though they are not a couple.

"Baby, you want to go out clubbing tonight?" Michael automatically places an order of Halibut for her and Boeuf a la Stroganoff for himself, the meal they always eat when they dine there.

"Do you have to ask? You know I'm always ready to club when I'm at home. What's happening at the law firm?" Tamara bites into her fish.

Michael takes a sip of wine before he answers. "Nothing much, the same old same old. We're going to hire a new senior attorney; her name is Amber Anderson."

"Well, well, fresh blood for you."

"I doubt it. She sounds like a nerd on paper, and that is not my type."

"You've not seen her yet?"

Michael cuts into his beef short rib. "No. Bruce has been interviewing her and will be the one to hire her, and I'll meet her when I get back next week."

"Speaking of attorneys, how is my favorite attorney, Randall, doing? I don't know why you won't hook me up with him, he's so fine."

Michael frowns and shakes his head 'no' at the same time. "What's with you and Randall always talking to me about hooking you two up? First, if you two really wanted to get together you would and second, why hook up two players when you both know it would not last because you both play too many games?"

"And they said we would never last and look at us now." Tamara laughs at her own self.

"Girl... get your bag so we can get out of here, it's time for us to party. You know you don't have a bit of sense."

They spend the rest of the night clubbing. They hit an after-work place for cocktails and then they head to several night spots before going back to Tamara's condo in Murray Hill on East 33rd. Her place is green and on the 12th floor with two bedrooms, two baths, and is about 1180 square feet. Tamara's guest room is decorated in a masculine chocolate brown because she says it's Michael's room, whereas her bedroom is all white and gold and very feminine.

Saturday, when they get up, both are dressed to go to another one of their favorite spots for breakfast. Michael is in cargo shorts, a t-shirt, and his favorite baseball cap. He is reading *The New York Times* when Tamara joins him dressed in all white.

"Good morning angel, and you look like my angel in all white, you ready to go get some breakfast?"

"I look good in white. I look just as pure as I am."

They laugh as they go out the door to catch a taxi to breakfast and after breakfast, they plan to spend the rest of the day hanging out in the city.

After sitting down at the restaurant, Michael gets up to go to the bathroom. "Order for me, baby, you know what I like."

She orders grilled bacon and eggs for him and Nova salmon and cream cheese for herself.

"How does your husband want his eggs, ma'am?"

"He's not my husband or boyfriend, and he wants them over easy. I'll have a cranberry juice and you can bring him orange juice."

"I'm sorry ma'am, but you two seem more married than most of the couples who come in here who are married."

Tamara shakes her head when Michael returns. He looks at her and wonders what is going on. "What's wrong? Why are you shaking your head? Did someone say or do something to you?" Michael looks around to see if he needs to put someone in check.

"Why is it that everywhere we go, people think we're married? It's like they don't even say *boyfriend*, they automatically think you're my husband."

Michael smiles and shows even white teeth with his sexy dimples. "Because we look good together and they can feel good vibes from us because we don't have the drama most men and women have when they're together. Once couples cross the line of friendship with each other, that's when all the drama begins. Baby, we have the best of both worlds. We have each other for male and female companionship without the drama."

"I know that's right." Tamara toasts her glass to his. "Thank God I have you in my life to keep me sane."

Sunday, they go to mass at Saint Patrick's Cathedral, then dinner at Tamara's parent's home on the exclusive East Side of Park Avenue that was decorated by her interior decorator mother, Adrienne Dominique Dubois-Walker, who is French. She is a petite size of five-five with olive skin tone, dark brown hair, and hazel eyes with high cheekbones. She lives in the property with her real-estate mogul husband, Thomas Walker, who is Cuban and African American and stands at six-four with black curly hair streaked with gray, dark brown eyes, and a cleft in his chin.

"*Bonjour.*" (hello) Adrienne kisses Tamara and Michael on both of their cheeks. "How long are you two going to be in New York?"

"*Bonjour. (hello)* We'll be here until Thursday and then we're going to L.A., and I'll be flying out Sunday from there to Europe to start my flights." Tamara hugs her father.

"When are you going to make an honest woman out of my daughter?" Thomas asks Michael every time he sees them together because, like everyone else, he does not understand their relationship.

"Daddy, how many times do I have to tell you Michael and I are just friends?"

"I'm going to keep asking until you make me believe you. You two will not make me believe you're not involved with each other. It is just not normal the relationship you have. You might as well go on and get married and give us some grandbabies." Thomas lifts his chin with one raised eyebrow.

Michael and Tamara laugh because after two years, they are used to this and sometimes, they just do not even try to explain their relationship. Just as dinner is going on, Tamara's brother, Joshua, comes in messing with everyone.

"What's up, brother-in-law? I didn't know you were in town. You want to hang out if your old lady will let you out to play?" Joshua Walker is a male version of Tamara with the same good looks at six-four, olive skin color, curly black hair, hazel eyes, and shadow beard with a sexy cleft in his chin like his dad. He lives a player lifestyle. An investment banker who is the CEO of his own firm, J.S. Walker and Associates, he plays around just as much as his sister and will say anything to anyone. He has called Michael his brother-in-law since a couple of years ago when all of them spent a weekend together in The Hamptons at his beach house.

"Hell yeah, let's go out tonight, baby... are you going with us?"

Before Tamara can answer, Joshua curls his lips. "Hell no. She's going to stay at home while us men hang out."

"Fine. I will call Alexandra to see if she wants to go out. I do not have to go out with you two. Alex and I will party all night long."

They finish dinner and Michael leaves with Joshua while Tamara goes to pick up Alexandra. Alexandra cannot believe they are going out while Michael is in town.

"Where is your husband? I can't believe he let you out tonight without him?" Alexandra Cunningham, also a flight attendant, is Tamara's other running buddy who also is like a sister, especially since Alexandra does not have any other family except an uncle, aunt, and one male cousin.

Since Dianna has gotten married and lives in L.A., she only flies part time, which leaves Tamara and Alexandra to hang out all the time. Alexandra is a beautiful woman who is five-ten with smooth dark brown skin, dark brown curly hair that comes to her shoulders, mysterious gray eyes, and a perfect body.

"Alex, why are you going there? You know Michael and I are just friends. Why is it so hard for everyone to believe that? He's out with my wild brother, Joshua."

"Because it is not normal the way you two act with each other, and why the hell did you let him go out with that fool? You know your brother doesn't have a lick of sense and is one of the biggest players in New York." Alexandra looks out the window because she is going to tell it to her straight; she turns back around with her arms crossed at her breasts. "But getting back to you and Michael, the chemistry between you two is strong, so strong there is a relationship that already exists and you two don't know it. You two are in love with each other and just have not faced it yet."

Tamara turns to her and gasps as she almost hit a post. "You've lost your mind. Michael and I have never crossed that line. We even help each other hook up with other people. We do not think of each other in that way at all. Trust me, if he were my man, do you think I would let him go out with my brother? And what's the deal between you two?"

"Mmm. You know I can't stand your brother and he can't stand me." Tamara's cell phone rings and before she can answer it, Alexandra tilts her head with narrow eyes. "I bet that's him checking on you now."

To prove her point, she hit speaker on the cell phone so Alexandra can hear it is not him. "Hello."

"Hey baby, you okay? Where are you? Do you want me to join you?"

Tamara forgets Alexandra is in the car with her when she hears his voice because it is so natural for her to be talking to him. "No, sweetheart. I'm fine, we're on our way to a club. You just hang out with Josh and have a good time and I'll see you when you get home."

She can hear her brother in the background yelling at Michael to get off the phone with his wife so he can enjoy his night out with the boys.

17

"Okay darling, talk to you when I talk to you."

"Talk to you when I talk to you." Tamara clicks off and looks over at Alexandra. "Shut up. Do not say a word."

Alexandra just smiles. "I rest my case."

They both get home around four in the morning again and go straight to bed... separately.

After their weekend, they start Monday off with them going to the tennis match at the US Open. Both love tennis and will try to go to some of the tennis matches in different cities during tennis season and even made it to the French Open last year in Paris. They stayed with Tamara's grandparents, Chantal and Philippe Dubois, who lives in the wealthy neighborhood of 16th arrondissement-Trocadero. Tamara loves Roger Federer and Michael loves Raphael Nadal. Just like there is competition between the two tennis champions, Tamara and Michael have the same competition when they have the chance to watch them play.

After spending the day at Flushing Meadows in Queens, they head back to Manhattan for dinner at The Carlyle Restaurant. While enjoying dinner, Tamara wants to talk about the future.

"Michael, do you ever want to get married?"

Michael almost drops his fork with the piece of filet mignon on it. "Where the hell did that come from?"

"I was just wondering because if you got married, your wife might not like the friendship we have with each other, and I don't want to lose you as a friend."

Michael stokes his goatee and then takes a sip of wine. "Well, since I have not thought about marrying anyone, the answer is simple. My wife, whoever she might be, would have to accept our friendship. But what about you? If you got married, I'm sure your husband will not want us hanging out and traveling like we do. I might be the one who loses my friend."

Tamara drinks some wine, tilts her head, and presses her lips together before she responds to him. "I guess neither one of us will get married because if someone cannot accept our friendship, they can't be in our lives as either your wife or my husband."

Michael toasts with his glass. "Here's to never getting married and keeping our friendship the way it is."

They both smile at each other because neither one wants to get married since they both love their freedom too much and value the friendship they have with each other. This is something they have never discussed but both know they feel the same way about and that is why they are such good friends: because they understand each other and want the same thing in life.

They spend the next couple of days hanging out throughout the city shopping, going to museums and art galleries. Wednesday, before they are to leave for L.A., they have dinner at LeCirque with Alexandra and Joshua, which is a trip because they spend most of the evening arguing with each other.

Michael orders the LeCirque salad for Tamara and the Spaghetti alla Citara with seafood for himself with an extra order on his plate of the spaghetti because he knows Tamara will eat off his plate as always when there is pasta.

"Why do you two continue to have this same fight over and over of how much a player Joshua is and how Alexandra is too stuck up?" Tamara takes her fork to eat spaghetti from Michael's plate.

"The same reason you always eat off of Michael's plate or he feeds you his food." Joshua stops eating to cross his arms and tilt his chin.

"What?"

"Tam, your interaction with each other is so comfortable, you don't realize what you're doing. That's the same way Alexandra and I interact with each other. We fight, and you two love." Joshua toasts his glass to Alexandra.

"That's right." Alexandra lifts her glass to his. "You two are married and don't even know it, whereas Joshua and I know we can't stand each other and are extremely comfortable with those feelings."

Michael, who has been quiet, finally speaks up. "Better to love than hate."

"You tell them, baby." Tamara toasts her glass to him.

They laugh because they all know they have different relationships that only they know and understand. The couples share a dessert with each other and end their night with the guys promising to hook up later and the girls knowing they will see each other on their flights.

The next day, Michael and Tamara eat a quick breakfast of croissants and tea so they can pack to head to the airport for L.A. Both love being in New York, but they both love the party scene in L.A. as well. Plus, they can see their best friends with a bonus of seeing Zachary and Kennedy, who both consider their niece and nephew.

"Baby, do you think you have enough luggage?" Michael laughs at all the Louis Vuitton luggage she is taking.

"You know I have to be cute, and it takes a lot to look good." Tamara adds another piece of luggage to the pile. "Anyway, you can't say anything, Michael, because you always travel with a lot of luggage too. You know we both must have plenty of clothes wherever we go."

Chapter Three

M ichael and Tamara's plane arrives in L.A. Thursday afternoon and Christina picks them up from the airport. They head to Dianna's house where both kids were waiting since Tamara was going to stay with James and Dianna and Michael is going to stay with his sister.

"How are my two favorite kids doing?" Michael asks while putting on his sunglasses.

"Great. They both are walking and getting into everything. What have you two been into besides partying?" Christina glances at them with the same light brown eyes and dimples her brother has. Shaking her head, she still does not understand their relationship.

"Now, how do you know we've been partying?" Tamara laughs, because everyone thinks that is all she and Michael do.

"Tamara, be for real. You know that's all you two do, especially when you two are in the same city together." Christina turns into the drive of the enormous home James and Dianna bought after marrying and having their daughter.

Dianna rushes out the door smiles. "Mikey and Tam, what's up? How is my favorite couple, even though you claim you're not a couple?"

Michael picks his other buddy up and swings her around, still not believing she's married and has a baby. Dianna was the biggest player of all of them, but that stopped when she got back with James after being apart from each other for fifteen years.

"Girl, you look good to be a mother and wife."

"I know." Never one to be modest about her looks, Dianna rubs her hand across her short black curly hair and smiles, still looking sexy.

Christina goes into the house to get the kids while they are standing outside talking. She returns with Zachary, who is a mini version of his uncle with jet black curly hair, the same light brown eyes Christina and Michael have, and those famous St. John dimples. Kennedy, who is the same age as Zachary, is the spitting image of her daddy. She has Dianna and James' coal black curly hair and James's skin color with brown bedroom eyes and his long eyelashes.

"What's up, Zach? You look more and more like your Uncle Michael every time I see you. You're going to break some hearts and be a playa just like me." He grabs him from out of his mother's arms as fat little chubby arms reach out to him.

Tamara picks up Kennedy who pulls her long hair squealing and laughing because just like her mother, she loves attention. They all go into the house to wait for James and Matthew, who are still at work, to join them later.

When Matthew and James get there, dinner is ready and Tamara is sitting in Michael's lap eating pasta as he feeds her off his plate. Standing there rubbing his shadow of a beard with narrow eyes, the first thing James says to them is, "You two still confused about your relationship?"

"No. We know exactly where we stand with each other." Tamara feeds Michael a piece of garlic bread.

Matthew the same height as James stands next to him and rolls his eyes. "I know this might be a dumb question, but why are you eating off his plate? I know James and Dianna have enough dinnerware and there is plenty of food, so why is it you don't have your own plate to eat from?"

"She's always watching her weight so when there are carbs around, which she loves, she never gets her own plate. I always get extra because I know she wants to eat from my plate."

"I swear man, you two married without really being married to each other." James fixes his plate, still not understanding their relationship.

They finish dinner and the women go into the great room with the kids to talk while the men go outside on the deck to catch up. Both parties are talking about the same thing: Tamara and Michael.

"Tamara, have you and my brother slept together yet?" Christina tilts her head and raises her eyebrows, knowing they have probably crossed that line.

"No. I keep telling everyone we're just friends. I got several guys I talk to when Michael don't run them away."

"Now why would Michael run away your guy friends?" Dianna glances sideways, wanting to know since they claim they do not have feelings for each other.

"You know Michael thinks he knows what's best for every-one." Tamara lies on the couch while Kennedy jumps up and down on her stomach.

"He never did that with any of my relationships. How about you, Dianna?" Christina asks.

"Nope."

It gets quiet because Tamara really does not know what to say. Her two friends sit there, looking at her because they are waiting for her to answer.

"Michael and I just have a close relationship no one seems to understand. I don't know why it's so strange to everyone because he's a man and I'm woman; we can really only be friends without crossing the line of sleeping with each other."

Dianna sips on a glass of wine. "Because most of the times when a woman and man are as close as you two are, they have slept together and are on their way to getting married. I don't care what you say, Tamara, the relationship you two have with each other is not normal."

"Whatever." Tamara throws Kennedy up in the air.

Meanwhile, Michael is being drilled by his two best friends outside. No one has ever got their relationship since last year when they kidnapped Dianna and when they first met in Memphis at Dianna's mother's birthday party.

"I'm sorry, man, but you and Tamara's situation... is crazy. You have all the benefits without the sex. I've never seen two people who keep up with each other, but not together." James frowns and sips on an after-dinner drink of brandy.

"You are just jealous because I'm not tied down to one woman like you. Tam is my best friend who is a female. If I had a new best friend named Leroy, you two wouldn't be putting me on the witness stand about my life." Michael sips on his drink of brandy as well while he lies on a deck chair, not paying any attention to them.

"If you had a new best friend names Leroy, I would hope you wouldn't be calling him *baby* and *darling* and him sitting in your lap while you feed him off your plate." James throws back his head and laughs.

Matthew, who is quiet while they go back and forth with each other, finally speaks up. "Usually, I do not go along with James but this time, I must agree with him. You and Tamara's relationship is different, and you treat her... let's say different from the way you treated me and James as your best friends."

"That's because you two are ugly."

They all laugh because Michael is stone crazy. "Seriously guys, we're just friends. For the last time, we bonded last year when we went through what we went through with Dianna's kidnapping, so let it go."

Matthew and James do not say a word, as strange as it might seem; maybe they are just friends like they have been preaching for a while.

Christina comes out to get her husband and brother so they can go home because it is time for Zachary to go to bed. They make plans for everyone to get together tomorrow at their house and then they are going to cookout Saturday at James and Dianna's before Tamara heads out to Europe Sunday morning.

As they are leaving, Tamara goes over to Michael and he whispers something in her ear. She burst out laughing then he grabs her to give her a hug, then kisses her gently on her forehead.

"I'll call you later, baby. Talk to you when I talk to you."

"Goodnight, sweetie. Talk to you when I talk to you."

Matthew, Christina, James, and Dianna stand there shaking their heads because they just do not get it. They are wild with everyone else and have not a care in the world, but with each other, they are two totally different people.

Friday morning at eleven, James, Dianna, Kennedy, and Tamara go over to Christina and Matthew's house to spend the day. The guys grill while the ladies fix all the side dishes. After eating, Tamara and Michael lay together on a lounge chair talking when James comes over to sit in a chair opposite of them because he must mess with them.

"So, Mrs. St. John, we were thinking about taking an all-boys trip next month; can your husband go?"

Tamara crinkles her nose and looks at him like he has two heads. "Dianna, come get your husband, he has lost what little mind he has."

Dianna comes over to see what is going on and knows her husband is up to something. "James, what did you say? Why don't you leave them alone; just because they confused about their relationship, you don't have to ride them about it."

James laughs and pulls his wife into his lap. "Baby, I just asked her if her husband can play with me and Matt next month if we decide to take an all-boys trip."

Matthew and Christina have joined them. Matthew who is laid back and cool cannot resist messing with his friend and brother-in-law too. "Man, he's on lock down more than we are. He probably can't go because his wife has other plans for him."

Michael loves to mess around and joins in on the fun. "Baby, can I hang out with the boys? Please baby, I'll be good."

Tamara love games as well. "Sure, baby, you can go as long as you'll be back in time for us to pick up the new curtains we ordered for our bedroom."

Christina shakes her head. "Something is wrong with all of you guys. James, you and Matt need to leave Michael alone and Michael, you and Tamara need to figure out your relationship with each other."

Saturday, everyone is at James and Dianna's house because the guys are going to watch the tennis match while the ladies and the kids go shopping. Christina is waiting for Dianna and Tamara to get ready, so she is watching tennis with the guys. Tamara has not seen or talked to Michael all day so when she comes downstairs after her and Dianna are dressed, she runs straight to him.

"Baby... did you miss me?"

Michael forgets he is watching the match and jumps up as soon as she walks in the room. "Yes, sweetheart. I'm sorry I did not call you this morning, but I got right up to go to the store with Matt to get the food for tonight's cookout. You look cute, baby."

"Okay. So, you call each other every morning when you wake up. Why don't you two just go on and get married?" James goes into his kitchen to get something to snack on.

Matthew replies before they can say anything. "They can't get married because they're just friends. Man, I don't know why you can't get that."

"I can't get it because they are not just friends. They just don't know or have not accepted what they are. Move out of the way because you two are blocking the match." James laughs at how Michael and Tamara both stand there looking.

Christina and Dianna go over to kiss their husbands and Dianna says, "Let's go, ladies. Tamara... go kiss her husband goodbye so we can shop until we drop."

"Do you need some money, baby?" Michael kisses Tamara on her forehead.

"No baby, I'm fine, I'll see you when I get back."

Michael stands there watching her until she disappears with Christina and Dianna. When he turns around, all he sees is two pairs of eyes staring at him. "What?"

Matthew just shakes his head and James stares at him and frowns. "I'm not joking this time. You two are in love and really do not know it. Michael, you need to face the fact that you got some serious feelings for that woman."

This is the first time Michael does not say one word. He sits down and watches the tennis match and says nothing because he does not know what to say.

Later that evening as they sit down to dinner, James asks, "Okay guys, it's just us here. You can go on and tell us what's really the deal between you two."

Michael laughs. "Okay, here's the truth. We are just friends. Why can't you people accept that?"

Matthew never looks up from his food. "Because it is not normal nor does it make any sense the relationship you two have with each other, but hey, if you say you are just friends then that's what it is."

James looks both directly in their eyes. "I'm not buying it. I know the both of you and for two people who do not do relationships, you two sure do an awful lot of relating with each other."

Christina gets in on the conversation. "I don't believe it either, but I agree with my husband. If that's what you two want us to believe, okay, you're just good friends."

The rest of the night, the friends debate about Michael and Tamara's relationship, then discuss their kids and work. Everyone must let it go about Tamara and Michael because until they face how they really feel about each other, it makes no sense to talk to them about their relationship.

Michael borrows Christina's car to take Tamara to the airport early Sunday morning because his flight is not leaving out until Sunday afternoon.

"Baby, how long are you going to be in Europe?"

"I'll be there for four days, then I fly back to the U.S. I will stop here in L.A. to pick up my luggage from Dianna then do a two-day flight to Florida, the Carolinas, and then back to New York. I'll be at home for five days before I go back out again to Europe."

They are at LAX and Michael comes around to help her out of the car and to get her bags. They stand there embracing each other because they know it will be a while before they see each other again because both are going to be busy with their schedules. This is something else other people do not know about them: they will go months sometimes without seeing each other. Sometimes, they might go weeks without even talking to each other, so they enjoy each other's company when they have the chance to hang out.

Michael runs his knuckle down her cheek. "I'm going to miss you, baby. I'm going to be tied up and traveling myself so we might not have time to talk for a while. You be good and stay out of trouble."

Tamara caresses his face. "I'm going to miss you too, baby. Try not to pick up no more stalkers because I will not have time to come whip some woman up to get her to leave you alone."

He laughs and bends down to kiss her lightly on the lips and says, like he always does when they part from each other, "Talk to you when I talk to you."

"Talk to you when I talk to you."

Chapter Four

Now back in Memphis, Michael was at his office Monday morning at six o'clock working extremely hard. He likes to get into the office early when no one else is there, especially when he has been out all week. Reviewing cases and preparing for a trip to New Orleans for a case, he is going there to work with the new attorney. He is taking her because he wants to see how she works. By nine o'clock, when everyone else was just getting there, his tie loose from his shirt collar, he leaves his office to go downstairs to get something to eat because he was starving. When he goes back upstairs, he stops by the new attorney's office but before going in, he hears her speaking with her assistant.

"So, Mr. St. John must not come into the office until around twelve. I guess if your daddy owns the company, you can do that."

"Mr. St. John has been here since six this morning. What time did you get here?" He walks through the door but stops right in the middle of his tracks. If this is Amber Anderson, they are going to have a problem. She is beautiful and not looking like the nerd he pictured her to be.

Amber gasps because she did not know he was outside of her door and now she knows he heard what she just said. When he walks in, she cannot believe he's Michael St. John, who is a cutthroat in the courtroom, because he is too fine. He looks like a player who is too busy partying hard rather than working in the office.

Coming out of his trance, he walks over to meet her. Standing there at five-eight with a golden skin color, dark brown eyes, naturally red curly hair to her shoulders, and a nice body, she extends her hand out to him. "Good morning, Mr. St. John. I'm Amber Anderson, it's nice to meet you."

Michael shakes her hand, not believing she is acting like she did not make the comment he overheard. "Please call me Michael, like everyone else. Welcome aboard and can you please come to my office by ten, so we can meet about this case I need you to work with me on in New Orleans?"

He walks out her office without looking back as she thinks to herself *arrogant bastard*. While walking to his office, he thinks to himself, *cocky woman*. Who the hell does she think she is to make that comment to her assistant about him? If he does not want to come in until twelve, he can. He can tell right now that they are not going to get along.

Amber is at his office at ten o'clock on the dot. "Michael, are you ready to go over the case?"

"Yes. This case is going to be tricky because the company we are representing has had some problems in the past but they really did not do this, this time. We got to be on top of our game." Michael looks over the file before he gives it to her to review.

"I'll take it home to go over it with a fine-tooth comb to be updated on what's going on with them."

"Great, we can meet tomorrow around one to plan our strategy before we go down there next week."

She nods and leaves to go back to her office to do research on the company and the lawsuit they are going to handle. Michael works on the rest of his cases and gets with Lisa about his court dates. He works until about seven that evening and before going downtown to his condo, he stops by his parent's house to say hello.

"Hey old man, what's going on?"

"Nothing much. What's up with you?"

"Where is Mom?"

"Now Michael, you know she don't get off work until nine o'clock tonight."

Michael laughs because her getting off work means her and her best friend, Doris, Matthew's mother, are at the mall or some store shopping until everything closes at nine. "Those two know they can shop. You would think they are tired of shopping by now."

"I wish. I would have a lot more money. Have you hired the new senior attorney yet?"

"Yeah, she started today. Very cocky and we'll probably bump heads."

"Really."

"Beautiful and cocky. I don't know what Bruce was thinking about hiring her, even though she looks good on paper. I'm not so sure I can deal with her personality."

Mike Sr. raises an eyebrow and looks at his son, who seems a bit shaken up by this woman He needs to call his buddy, Matt Sr., so they can check things out. She just might be a candidate who can make him slow down to be with just one woman.

"I just stopped by on my way home. I'm not hanging out tonight because I've been in the office since six this morning. I am tired, especially since I just got back from New York and L.A. Your grandchildren are growing like weeds."

"I bet. I can't wait to see them." Even though Zachary is his only grandchild, he considers Kennedy his granddaughter because Dianna is like a daughter to him. As soon as Michael leaves, he calls his partner, Matt Sr.

"He seems really upset by her."

"Do you think they got off on the wrong foot?"

"Maybe; he said he can't deal with her, but he also said she was beautiful."

"You think we should check things out?"

"I say we stop by our old office tomorrow to meet the new attorney and see what's going on... with our on two eyes."

"You know Michael might not want to mix business and pleasure."

"True, but if she's fantastic looking, you know he can't resist a good-looking woman."

"Let's meet in the morning to play a round of golf about eight and then go by the office."

"That will work. I'll see you in the morning."

"See you in the morning."

Chapter Five

Michael feels better after a good night's sleep. He stopped on the way home to get something to eat, took a hot shower, turned off his cell phone so it would not disturb him, and slept for twelve hours straight. He was now ready to deal with everyone, including Amber. On his commute from downtown to his office, he thinks maybe she is not cocky and he was just tired from his trip.

Lisa and Michael have a twelve o'clock meeting but before their office meeting starts, Lisa needs to talk to her boss about something personal. They have been together for five years and it is easy to talk to Michael about anything, but she is not so comfortable to talk to him about this subject.

Lisa clears her throat. "Michael, before we get started, can I talk to you about something concerning a personal situation?"

"Sure, what's up?"

"Well... I really don't know how to bring this up because you've been so good to me and I appreciate everything you have done for me, but—"

Michael cocks his head to the side. "What is it, Lisa? You know you can talk to me about anything."

"Michael, is there any way I can get a raise? My ex-husband

has stopped paying child support and I need more money to take care of my two boys. With everyday household expenses and their schooling, I am barely making it. I know I had a raise six months ago, but is there any way you might consider another one for this year?"

"Girl, don't scare me like that. I thought you were going to tell me you have found another job. You know I could not function without you in my life. If all you want is a raise, that's an easy fix. I will tell Bruce as soon as I finish with my meeting with Amber to give you a twenty-five percent raise. Is that okay?"

"Thank you so much. I just need more money to live off. Also, I need all your receipts and expense report, so I can turn them into accounting. I also put your American Express, car payment, and mortgage bill in your tray for you to pay. Michael, your American Express Black Card bill is crazy. I cannot believe you charged up as much as you did. Now, let us go over your schedule."

After going over his schedule, Lisa wants to make sure nothing overlaps. "Are you and Tamara going anywhere soon? I need to make sure your schedule is clear if you are."

Michael stretches his long legs out from the small conference table in his office. "No, we both will be working hard for the next few weeks, so we won't be hanging out. She is flying hard, so I will not see her for a while. You know I'll be in New Orleans with Amber for the next two weeks working on this case."

"I got it, but do you need me to block your schedule for when you get back? Because if you're going right back out, you need to pay your Amex bill right away."

"Well... it depends on how this trip goes. If this woman doesn't work my last nerve, I might be around but if it's a rough trip, I might have to hop a jet and go somewhere." Michael laughs while Lisa stands there and shakes her head at her boss.

"You're crazy. Amber will be here in a minute so try to be nice to her; she just started and does not know you do not have a lick of sense. Thanks again, Michael, for the raise."

Michael laughs because everyone knows he is crazy in his

office, but they also know he is no joke when it comes to business. He puts back on his suit jacket then straightens his black, red, and gray silk tie for his one o'clock meeting.

"You ready to go over everything?" Amber comes into his office with a solid black dress on with sexy pumps that make her legs look longer and serve as a distraction to Michael.

He smiles. "I'm ready. Did you go over everything, and do you think you will be ready when we go to New Orleans?"

"I went over it and I have a question. Do we really want to take this case?"

Michael crosses his arms across his broad chest. "Are you questioning my judgment on taking the case?"

"I'm not saying you made the wrong decision, but maybe it's not the best decision."

Michael presses his lips together and looks her up and down then lets her have it. They exchange words until it turns into a yelling session.

"You just got here, so how are you going to tell me we might not want to take this case?"

"I'm just saying they might not be worth us dealing with them because they have had problems in the past."

"Amber, that's not your call. You just work here, and it's not your decision on what cases we take. That's my call and Bruce's call. You're just assigned cases to work on."

Everyone in the office stops because they have never heard Michael get angry. Just as the screaming match gets louder and louder, in walks Mike Sr. and Matt Sr.

"What's going on?" Mike Sr. is wide-eyed, not believing his son is screaming at some woman while she is screaming back at him in his office.

"Sound like someone is not getting along. You think we better go in there before they kill each other?" Matt Sr. smiles because he knows his friend is right again.

They walk into Michael's office while he and Amber are in each other's faces shouting like they are at home fighting over the kids.

"You must be the new attorney? I'm Michael St. John Sr., the owner, and this is Matthew Phillips Sr., the other owner. Michael, I can't believe you two are having a disagreement about something."

"She feels maybe we don't need to take this case." Michael turns his head away from Amber with his nostrils flaring because no one has ever made him this mad, especially at work.

"Well, let me see the case and Mike and I will decide if you need to take it, if it will keep you two from killing each other." Matt Sr. goes behind Michael's desk to look at the file.

"Do what you want and let me know. I'm out of here." He looks at Amber with throbbing veins in his neck and walks out of his office.

Amber has tears in her eyes because she realizes being such a strong independent woman and a prosecuting attorney has pushed the wrong buttons with her new boss. She knows sometimes, she goes too far, but that was what made her a great prosecutor. But now, she is not working with hard criminals anymore; this is a different type of law.

"I'm sorry, Mr. St. John and Mr. Phillips. I know I get carried away and it seems I keep putting my foot in my mouth with Michael. I'm sure he's probably ready to send me back to Atlanta by now." Amber has a lump in her throat and holds back her tears.

Mike Sr. and Matt Sr. look at each other and smile. They know it is the right time to put their scheme into place because she might be the woman he needs to date.

Mike Sr. speaks up first. "Don't worry about it. I know my son and if you apologize to him and tell him what you just told us, he will forget everything. Michael is too carefree to stay mad."

She looks at Matt Sr. and he nods his head in agreement with Mike Sr. "Go find him to straighten things out."

"It looks like we have found the woman Michael can date that might lead to something."

"If they don't kill each other first."

"Yeah, but that's why I know my son would be perfect for her.

His looks and money do not excite her, and that's exactly what he needs."

"You know, his good looks have always been his downfall. He is so used to women flocking to him because of his looks and status."

"That's why they are the perfect fit for each other. She's the only woman I have ever known to make him mad."

"What's our next step?"

"When they get back from New Orleans, we'll be in L.A. visiting the kids. Maybe we need to have a meeting with Michael to tell him to bring Amber out to L.A. with him to discuss a case that would be perfect for them to work on together."

"I got it. Get them away from Memphis and away from work where they can relax with each other, especially after a work trip together in New Orleans."

"That's it."

"This is going to be fun with your crazy son."

Michael stands in the kitchen down the hall from his office watching the sports channel, trying to relax his mind after his round with Amber. He cannot believe she made him lose his cool like that. He must admit she could hold her own. If she had not made him so angry, he might admire her a little.

"Hello, my name is Amber Anderson and I've put my foot in my mouth."

Michael turns around to see this beautiful woman standing there looking like a scared little girl who has lost their best friend. He cannot do anything but smile, showing his famous dimples.

"Michael, I am so sorry. Being a prosecutor for so long, I'm so used to tearing everything apart to win my case. I forgot this is a different type of law." She drops her head, then looks up. "That's why I wanted this job because the law I have been practicing has made me become so cynical in my personal life when I'm really a fun person. There are reasons I wanted to leave Atlanta, and one of them was to stop practicing the type of law I have practiced since I got out of law school. I am pleased with my career, but it has somewhat destroyed my personal life. I am so sorry and really want this job."

Michael gives a slightly close-lipped smile because he was not expecting her to be so apologetic. "Amber, I just think we got off on the wrong foot. I overheard you saying I come in late because my dad owns the firm. I think you think of me as a spoiled rich kid who never works and just travels and plays around. I travel a lot and play around, but I also work ridiculously hard. Sometimes, I'm here fifteen to eighteen hours a day and believe it or not, I have a full office in my condo downtown, because sometimes I work in the middle of the night."

Amber's mouth flies open because he states everything she thought. "Can we start over? I would love to work this case with you if you will still have me."

"I think you would be a great asset to this case, and I think we're going to knock them dead." He reaches out to shake her hand.

She put her hand into his and for a moment, they stare at each other before letting go. And of course, who sees the interchange?

"It seems like you two have worked it out." Mike Sr. raises one eyebrow at the couple.

"We looked over the case and we think it would be good to help this insurance company get their name back clear, and you two will be the perfect ones to do it." Matt Sr. knew they were going to work it out because there seems to be some attraction between them.

Once Michael leaves the kitchen to go back to his office and Amber leaves to go to hers, they have a cup of coffee, basking in their glory.

"Did you see the handshake?"

"Yeah. Looks like to me they had a silent peace offering, which means it could lead to something else."

"I know my son and with her attitude and good looks, I give him two weeks and I guarantee you he'll be asking her out to dinner, and not for business."

"I bet when they get back from New Orleans, they'll start seeing each other on a personal basis."

"And we're going to help get it started by getting both out to L.A. when they get back. If they win the case, which I believe they will, they'll be in a good mood and both will be ready for some relaxation."

"Good plan. Back from a hard trip and away from business will do the trick."

"Let us go. I feel like another round of golf. What about you?"

"I always feel good once a plan falls into place. I'm ready for another round, too."

Chapter Six

One of Tamara's permanent flight routes is to Europe. Paris, France is the city she flies into more than anywhere else there. Paris is like a second home to her because she is half-French and would come to Paris as a child every summer to see her grandparents, uncles, aunts, and cousins. Since going to Paris as much as she does, she met a French business executive, Francois Xavier Renaud IV, who is senior vice president over finance at Moet Hennessy-Louis Vuitton, better known as LVMH. They have been dating for the last three months and for her, that is serious because she usually does not date anyone that long. He is charming, successful, rich, and a lot of fun.

"*Bonjour.*" (Hello)

"*Bonjour.*" (Hello)

"*Comment allez-vous?*" (How are you)

"*Je vais bien.*" (I'm fine)

"Darling... are you going to be here long?" Francois' smile shows even white teeth under a goatee and moustache. He stands at six-one with blue eyes and coal black hair.

"Yes. I have a layover here for four days, so I can spend time in this beautiful city and with you." Tamara smiles at him because on top of everything else, he is fine and she loves fine men. "Since I left L.A. and Michael two weeks ago, it has been nonstop for me. I've not been back to New York in a month."

"So, you were in L.A. with Michael?" Francois frowns because like everyone else, he does not understand their relationship. This is a major issue for him because he wants a serious relationship with her but feels Michael is the third wheel. She has told him several times there is nothing between her and Michael, but she also talks about him all the time and calls him while they are together.

"Of course, silly, I told you Michael came to New York to hang out with me there for some days and then we flew to L.A. to see everyone before I started all my flights."

"Hmm." He rolls his eyes, sighing at the same time.

"Francois, don't take that attitude." Tamara's hands go up, tired of defending her and Michael's relationship. "This is the last time I'm going to tell you we're just friends. Now, I want to enjoy my time here with you."

They get into his 750LI Black BMW to drive to his home, which is in the 16th arrondissement-Tocadero, a conservative residential neighborhood for the wealthy on the right bank of the River Seine and is also around the corner from where her grandparents live. She makes a mental note to call them in the morning to run around there to see them before she flies back out. After dropping off her bags, they go to their favorite restaurant, LePavillon de la Grande Cascade on Alle'e de Longchamp for a meal. They share a bottle of wine and talk about them and what direction they want to take their relationship in. Francois wants to make love to her and asks her to join him in his bedroom.

"Tamara, I want to make love to you, and I think it's time you join me in my bedroom... please."

"I am going to think about it... Francois, because I want to make sure we are doing the right thing and not rushing into anything. Tonight, I'll sleep in your guest room to think about things and then we'll see about tomorrow."

Francois grabs her hand and kisses it. "Thank you, my love, that's all I can ask for."

When they get back to his house, Tamara goes to his guest room to sleep like she has always done when she visits him. She must decide if she wants to take their relationship to the next level. She hopes she is making the right decision so she calls her buddy, Michael, to see if it is the right thing to do since she has not talked to him in a couple of weeks.

Michael is in New Orleans with Amber and is enjoying her company. They have a lot in common and she is good in the courtroom. They have developed their daily routine with each other, both having a cappuccino for breakfast before they head to the Louisiana Supreme Court building. At lunch, they both have also fallen in love with a traditional New Orleans Po'boys sandwich. Every day, they eat the sandwich that comes on a soft crust of French bread with lean boiled ham and well-done roast beef in garlic gravy with crispy fried shrimp. They have been in New Orleans for two weeks in court to work with the insurance company to prove an attorney has overbilled them for work he has not performed. Everything is going well with them, personally and business-wise. To be honest, he likes her.

This is the last night before they wrap up their case. They are having a typical New Orleans dinner after work when Michael's cell phone rings. He looks and see it's Tamara, so he excuses himself from Amber to take the call.

"Hey baby. What's going on, and where are you?"

"Darling, I'm in love."

"What! What the hell are you talking about?"

"I'm in Paris and I've been seeing a French business executive every time I come here, and I think I'm going to see him exclusively."

"A name, Tamara."

"His name is Francois Xavier Renaud IV, and he's fine as hell. Where are you?"

"I'm in New Orleans with Amber at dinner."

"Who the hell is Amber?"

"My new senior attorney."

"Hmm. I know that voice tone and if she's the one you said was a nerd, you don't sound like you're out with a nerd. A nerd would not be at dinner with you at ten o'clock at night."

"She is beautiful, but we're not talking about her, what about Frenchy?"

"Do not change the subject on me, Michael St. John, do you like her?"

"Yes."

"Well, I like Francois, so it looks like we both have found someone to settle down with."

"I didn't say all that and don't you rush into anything. You don't even know him."

"I've known him for three months, how long you have known Ms. Amber?"

"I will not have this conversation with you right now. I'll call you back later. Talk to you when I talk to you."

"Talk to you when I talk to you."

When Tamara hangs up, she does not feel right and she does not know why. She really does not care Michael is in New Orleans with his new attorney because she is in the city of love with a fine man, but she still is not happy after their conversation.

Back in New Orleans, Amber looks uncomfortable with hearing Michael's conversation. She heard her name mentioned, so she does not think she will cross the line to ask who he was talking to.

"Was that your sister?"

"No, that was my best friend, Tamara."

Michael's mood has changed because he was not expecting a phone call like that from Tamara. He does not understand why it is bothering him that she claims she is in love. Maybe because for the two years they have known each other and hung out, she has never said she even liked anyone, let alone said she was in love. He will call her back when he gets to his room.

"Are you all right? It seems like your mood has changed since the conversation."

"I'm sorry, Amber, but she calls out the blue stating she's in love with some French dude. You don't understand, Tamara is wild and for her to call me from Paris talking about she's in love is strange."

"Well, maybe she has fallen hard and just wanted to share it with her friend."

"Who knows with Tamara, but let's not let her spoil our evening. I'll talk to her later."

Amber gives him one of her sexy smiles, but behind it she feels there is more to it concerning Michael and Tamara. She does not know if they used to mess around with each other and are now friends or if they are still messing around with each other now and he is lying to her about who she really is. She likes Michael, so she will wait and see what will happen between them next. Michael walks Amber to her room and for the first time, he kisses her on her cheek and tells her he will see her in the morning for breakfast because tomorrow is their last day there. As soon as he gets in his room, he picks up his cell phone to call Tamara back.

"Baby... why are you not answering the phone? Call me right back."

For the first time since they have been friends, Tamara does not call him right back after the message he left. He cannot believe she does not return his call; the only time she does not call right back is when she is in the air, and he knows she is not in the air because he just talked to her an hour ago.

Michael's cell phone finally rings two hours later and it is Tamara.

"You back from your date?"

"That's not important. Who is this guy, and are you sure you're in love with him?"

"Your date is important, and why don't you want to talk about it?" Tamara half-smiles, wondering what really happened between him and the new attorney.

Michael lets out a deep breath. "Tamara, we were having

dinner, that's all. You're the one who calls me talking about you are in love. Just because you've been seeing someone for a while, that doesn't mean you're in love."

"Well...I might not be in love, but I have been seeing him for three months."

Michael strokes the nape of his neck, not believing she has kept this from him. "He must not be that important if you're just now telling me about him, and three months is not long enough to be talking about you're in love with someone."

"Three months is a long time for me. You know I rarely talk to anyone longer than a month."

"Yeah, it might be long for you, but it's still not long enough to get seriously involved with anyone. You really don't know this guy."

"You really don't know Amber either."

"I didn't call you telling you I was in love with Amber, so don't go there."

"Yeah, but you said you like her."

"I might have said I like her, but you call me telling me you are in love with Francois."

Tamara rubs her eyes because she does not want to fight with him. "We'll talk about Francois and Amber when I get back. Talk to you when I talk to you."

"You got that right we'll talk about them both when you get back to the States. Talk to you when I talk to you."

Chapter Seven

Michael and Amber head back to Memphis after winning the lawsuit, and Michael asks her out to dinner so they can talk personally. They are going out tomorrow night. Amber feels there must be nothing going on between him and Tamara because he wants to take her out, and not for business.

Back in Paris, Tamara talks to Francois about how Michael was out with Amber and how he claims she is a nerd.

"I'm telling you. I know my friend and the way he talks about her, she is not a nerd."

Francois' narrow eyes looks up from the paper he is reading. "Why do you care?"

"What do you mean, why do I care? He's my friend and I want to make sure he's all right."

"Darling, it looks like to me you care too much. Michael is free to be with anyone who he wants to be with, or is he? You two are too much involved in each other lives and I will not have him in our lives with our relationship."

Tamara is furious. How dare he talk to her that way? One word led to another and now they are in a full-on fight. She will not let him separate her from one of her best friends, and he says

46

he will not have another man in his relationship. He tells her he has always felt from day one she talked about, talked to, and sees Michael St. John too much.

Tamara runs out the room crying because she really does not understand why her and Michael's relationship is such a problem for everyone. She is tired of defending it and even tired of explaining it. Upset and lonely, she does what has become second nature to her: she calls Michael. Even though she has not talked to him since their last conversation, which was not that great, and it's one o'clock in the morning in Memphis, she knows he will talk to her.

A sleepy Michael hears his cell phone ringing in his sleep. He's tired from traveling and working late in the office because he goes there straight from the airport.

"Hello."

"Michael...it's me."

He sits straight up because he knows something is wrong. "Baby, what's wrong? Where are you?"

"I'm still in Paris and Francois and I just had a big fight... and Michael, he hurt my feelings."

Michael jumps up out of his bed, muscles tense. "He didn't hit you, did he? Because if that jackass has touched you, I'm on the first flight out of here."

"No, he didn't touch me, he just said some mean things to me about us. He doesn't want me to hang around you as much as I do."

"Baby, come home. I do not want you anywhere where you are unhappy. I never want to get a phone call in the middle of the night where you are crying. You know I cannot take it when you cry. Do you think you two will make up, or do you think you should just walk away?" he holds his breath, hoping and praying she will not stay there because she needs to walk away from him.

"I'm going to walk away from it. He does not understand the relationship between you and me because he feels we are too close. He said he does not want you in our relationship and that I talk about and see you too much. The way he feels about our friendship, I cannot possibly be with him because I'll not let anyone come between us."

Michael grins from ear to ear. "Baby, you don't need anyone in your life who will try to keep us apart. If any woman were to say that about you, I would be out of there. Men and woman can come and go, but genuine friends are hard to find. We knew from day one what we have with each other is special and people just do not understand it, nor do they know what we went through to become this close to each other. Come home, baby. Come home here to Memphis and stay with me for a couple of days before you must fly back out."

Tamara's tears well in her eyes with a shaky voice because he is the one person who understands her. "I'm going to call the airport right now and get a flight out. I want to see you and be there with you, sweetheart."

"And I want you here with me too, baby. You still have your key to my condo, so it doesn't matter what time you get in. Even if I'm tied up, you can just come straight here."

"Yes, I have my key and I'll come straight there from the airport. Talk to you when I talk to you, and Michael...I love you."

"Talk to you when I talk to you, and I love you too."

As soon as she makes her reservation to fly out tomorrow afternoon, Dianna calls her to see what is going on. She tells Dianna what just happened with her and Francois and after talking to Michael, she will be on a flight that arrives in L.A. at one tomorrow, then she heads to Memphis.

"Michael was ready to come here to kick his ass. He told me I did not need to be with anyone who does not understand our friendship because he said he would not be with anyone who cannot accept me as his friend. He said since I have a key to his condo to just come straight there when I get in, even if he's tied up."

Dianna has not changed one bit and says exactly what is on her mind. "Tamara, that's crazy as hell. First, why do you have a key to Michael's condo in Memphis? And no one is going to be with either of you with this sick relationship you two have. Don't you think it is strange you two turn to each other for everything and neither one of you have been in a serious relationship with anyone else in the past two years?"

"First, I have a key to his condo and he has a key to mine because if we're in each other's city and we're not there, we always have a place to stay. And no, we do not have a sick relationship because we understand and tell each other everything. Just because we have not slept together and have not claimed a boyfriend and girlfriend status, everyone thinks our relationship is so different. Michael and I utterly understand each other, and we also respect each other. Dianna, you of all people should understand that Michael and I have nothing going on with each other. He's one of my best friends, like you and Alexandra. He's just a guy and no one wants to accept it because he's a guy."

"Okay. But you need to face that you have some deep feelings for Michael and he has those same deep feelings for you. You two play with everyone else's feelings and do not give a damn but with each other, he cannot make a move without you, and you cannot make a move without him, and that's more than just being best friends. If you two do not get it together, you'll never have a relationship with anyone else. No one will deal with the relationship that is between you two because he's a man and you're a woman, and it's not normal. Either you two need to face what is really going on with each other or stop acting like you're married to each other so you can have a relationship or maybe have a marriage with someone else. I am not getting into this with you anymore. Have a safe trip and call me later."

Dianna goes into the bedroom where her husband, James, is waiting for her after she put their daughter down for the night. "Listen to this. Tamara is breaking up with her French boyfriend because he is tired of hearing about Michael, and Michael told her to come home because she does not have to deal with that. And did you know they have keys to each other's condo? Baby, I am telling you, something is wrong in the head with both of my best friends. Why is it that everyone else can see they have serious feelings for each other, and they can't see it?"

49

James shakes his head back and forth while he reaches out for his wife. "Baby, I told you last year they have feelings for each other. Here is the deal: Tamara and Michael are in love with each other and really do not know it. And until they figure it out, they are going to keep going around in circles and not be with anyone else because they both are going to block it with the feelings they have for each other."

Dianna cuddles up with her husband. "I wonder how long they're going to go on like this."

James takes his wife's sweats off to make love to her. "Who knows? Right now, I do not want to think or talk about them. I want to make love to my wife."

The next day, Michael does not hear from Tamara, but he is not worried because he knows she is probably flying and trying to connect to get to Memphis. Paris is not a short flight, and she must come in through L.A. or New York then get a connecting flight to Memphis. He is going to keep his plans for dinner with Amber because whatever time she gets in. She has a key to his condo if he is not there. Michael calls his dad to tell him about New Orleans and surprised his parents, Matthew's parents, James's parents, along with Dianna's mother Cathy are all out in L.A. visiting their grandchildren. His dad is trying to talk him into coming out there and bringing Amber so they can discuss some business, and also so she can meet his family.

"Dad, I just got back from being out of town for two weeks and I have a lot to do around here, plus Amber doesn't need to come out there. Tell me about the case and I'll discuss it with her at dinner tonight."

"You and Amber going out for dinner tonight for business or pleasure?"

"Pleasure. I enjoy talking with her. She's smart and beautiful."

"Well... we'll talk about it later. Have a nice dinner son."

When Mike Sr. gets off the phone Matthew and James ask who Amber was and why is he trying to get Michael to bring her out there. He tells them she is the new senior attorney who he bumped heads with when she first joined the firm after discussing a case, but now they are going out to dinner together.

James laughs. "It will not work."

Matt Sr. asks, "Why do you say that?"

"Because of Tamara."

"Who's Tamara...not his friend?" Charlie, James's dad, narrows his eyes and squints because he is completely in the dark.

"I thought him and Tamara were just friends. Why would his relationship with someone else not work because of her?" Matt Sr. tilts his head and shrugs his shoulders, lost about their relationship.

"Who's Tamara?" Charlie asks again.

"Tamara is Michael's girlfriend, who is really not his girlfriend at least that's what he says, but she really is. You see guys," Matthew smiles with his eyes and mouth to clear things up. "Michael and Tamara will never be with anyone else because no one in their right mind would put up with how they are with each other. They say they are just friends, and, in their minds, they think they are, but they really are in a relationship with each other. I'm telling you it's twisted."

"It's as twisted as a relationship can be. They keep up with each other and tell each other everything. I bet you could call Michael right now and he can tell you where Tamara was and what she is doing. I'm telling you if you ever need to know where your son is, Uncle Mike, just call Tamara." James laughs at all three men's expressions.

Just as Mike Sr. and Matt Sr. are going to ask them to elaborate some more, they hear the women screaming out loud and when they run into the great room. They all are standing there pointing to the TV.

Chapter Eight

Michael is sitting in Fleming's restaurant on Poplar Ave with Amber having a nice romantic dinner. He has his cell phone on the table because he is waiting for Tamara to call him to let him know she has made it to Memphis. Amber laughs at Michael because he is being his charming, funny self. He differs totally from when he is in the office and this Michael, Amber likes.

Michael's cell phone rings and he picks it up off the table to answer as he looks at the ID, thinking it is Tamara, but it is his sister Christina. "Excuse me, but this really is my sister Christina."

"Hey Chris, what's up?"

"Michael," Christina with a lump in her throat. "Michael, are you looking at TV?"

"No, I'm out on a date, why?"

"Michael."

"What is it Chris, what's going on?"

"Michael, there was a plane crash and Tamara was on the flight coming into L.A. from Paris that crashed."

Michael hollers out and everyone turns around in the restaurant to look at him. "Is she okay, did she survive?"

"We don't know."

"I'm on my way out there. I'll be there on the next flight out." Michael's pale face gets up from the table and tells Amber. "I have to go, Tamara's plane crashed."

He walks out the restaurant and heads straight to Memphis International Airport, leaving her there and not caring how she was going to get home or what she thought. All he knows is that he is more afraid than he has ever been in his life. Michael gets lucky with the first flight going out to L.A. He does not have to wait but thirty minutes before Delta is leaving out and they have one seat left in first class. He arrives in L.A. at six o'clock and goes straight to Christina and Matthew's house. When he walks in, everyone looks at him.

"Is she okay? Did she survive?"

No one says a word until Matthew speaks up. "Right now, they're saying no one survived."

Michael screams out. "NO!" He collapses onto the floor on his knees, sobbing. "She can't be gone. I love her. I love her."

Everyone just stands there and his two best friends go to him to form the surrounding bond they have always done when one of them is in trouble. They have stuck by each other through everything, and Matthew and James never thought they would see Michael break down like this about any woman. All the parents and his sister, Christina, do not know what to do because even though they have not known Tamara as long as Dianna has, they know something is special between her and Michael and now she could be gone for good.

Michael, Matthew, and James stand at the same French doors they stood at last year with James when they kidnapped Dianna and James thought he would not see her again.

"Man, I didn't know how much I loved her. I did not realize that I was so much in love with her until right now. We had said we were just friends for so long that even I believed it. We have never kissed each other or made love, so it kept our relationship on the friendship level, and she was just in my life as the person I turned to for everything. Now, I know what actual love is, it is not about having sex because you can have sex with anyone. We had something so deep with each other and you can't get that with just anyone. I know I was the one who told her to leave Paris and come home. When she told me she was going to get serious with that French dude, I got pissed off and if I had been honest with myself and her, she would not have been in France with him because we would not have been playing this game we have been playing with each other. It's funny because we've always just said to each other when we depart 'talk to you when I talk to you' but this time, she said something she has never said before. For the first time, she said *I love you*. Those were the last words she said to me, and I told her I love you too. We had never said that to each other before."

Matthew and James do not know what to say. For him to have lost his only genuine love while he is just realizing he loves her must be the worst pain anyone can go through. Matthew lost Christina to her business and thought she was dying when their dad told him she would not make it. James was without Dianna when his former assistant had her kidnapped and he thought he would not see her again. Both cannot imagine being told the loves of their lives dying in a plane crash; it was so final. That means she's gone and he will never have the chance to see her again.

The three men stand there when Dianna rushes over to the door. "Michael, Mr. Walker just called to tell me they have found Tamara's body, but he's waiting to see if she made it. No one knows. They told them to come to the hospital right away but will not tell them anything over the phone. Let us go to the hospital."

Michael looks wide eyed because he thought they knew for sure she was gone. "You mean she might have made it?"

"That's just it, no one knows. We need to get to the hospital right away."

Cathy said she will stay there with the grandchildren because they do not need to go to the hospital and for them to call her to keep her posted. Everyone else jumps into their cars to head to Cedar Sinai Medical Center. When they get there, people and the news teams are everywhere, because Tamara is not the only person on the plane, so people are there trying to park and find out about their loved ones. They park and every entrance they go to they cannot get in until Matthew sees their friend, Detective Ryan Fields. Ryan is from Memphis too and had gone to law school with Matthew, James, and Michael. He is the one who found Dianna last year when they kidnapped her. When he sees his friends, his heart is racing.

"No... please don't tell me Dianna was on that flight?" He knows Dianna is a flight attendant while his heart rate drops completely.

"No. Tamara was on the flight and we're trying to get in to find out if she made it." James pulls Dianna up to him so Ryan can see she is okay.

"Michael, that's your lady? Come on, I'll escort you guys in personally." Ryan shows his badge to the police officers who are stopping people at the door if they are not immediate family.

For the first time in two years, Michael does not say Tamara is not his lady. Usually when someone says that to them, both always say they are just friends, but not tonight. She is not just his lady, she is the love of his life.

It is crazy in the hospital. People are everywhere trying to get information and they are still bringing people in from the plane crash. They look for Tamara's family and do not see anyone until Michael spots Joshua, Tamara's brother. They run to each other and hug. Joshua calls him brother-in-law because he did not believe they were not in a relationship and, like everyone else, he does not keep asking them about it. He would introduce him to people as his brother-in-law.

"How are you, man?" Joshua is more solemn than Michael has ever seen him.

"I love her, Josh. I can't lose her, she means the world to me."

He looks him dead in the eyes. "I know you do, and I've always known you two loved each other, you two just didn't know it."

They all head to where Tamara's parents are and after everyone meets everyone, all they can do is wait. Christina stands right by her brother holding his hand, and she keeps telling him she is going to make it; she just hopes and prays she is right. They come in and call a family name to tell them the good or bad news. Finally, after waiting three hours, they call for Tamara Walker's family. They all rush over to the nurse and when she tells them, "She's alive."

She cannot tell them her condition because the doctor has not got to her yet, but she can tell them she made it; she is one of the few who survived. They all are hugging each other because she is alive. Michael does not care what condition she is in as long as she is alive. He has not lost the love of his life.

They go back to waiting until a doctor can come out to tell them her condition. After another three hours of waiting, the doctor finds the Walker family to tell them the condition of Tamara.

He looks exhausted and takes them into the conference room where he can talk to them in private. "You guys are an incredibly lucky family. Ms. Walker has acute hypothermia because she was in the water longer than the human body should be in cold water. Her body temperature is 89, which is below what it's supposed to be of 98.6. She has a severe case because with the temperature of 89, her blood pressure, pulse, and respiration rates all decrease. She was in respiratory failure when she came in, but now she is okay and not in respiratory failure anymore; she is just semiconscious. What we have done is a blood rewarming where her blood drawn, warmed, and recirculated in her body, and we also have her on warm intravenous fluids which is a solution of saltwater that is being injected into her veins to help warm the blood as well. There is a nasogastric tube in her to keep her stomach empty and she is on the medicine Glucose and Thiamine. So far, she does not have pneumonia or kidney failure, which is great. Of course, we are running different tests to make sure nothing else is wrong."

"By her being semiconscious and not in a coma, she keeps coming in and out. With everything we have done and are doing, it should get her body temperature back to normal. Where is her husband, Michael? That is the only thing she has said when she comes to is his name."

Michael steps forward. "I'm not her husband."

"I'm sorry, her boyfriend."

Everyone looks when he drops his head. "I'm not her boyfriend either. We're just good friends."

The doctor gets up and smiles. "Well, son... I have been a doctor for a long time and after what she has been through and your name is the only thing that comes out of her mouth, you two are more than just friends. I am looking at you and you look too stressed out to just be friends. I think you have found your soulmate. Finding someone can come in all different ways at different times. Would you like to see your friend since she's been asking for you?"

Everyone follows the doctor back to the room Tamara is in and they decide, including her parents, to let Michael go in first. When he walks in, he stops at the door and his knees go weak when he sees her laying there so still with all the machines surrounding her. He finally gets enough strength to walk over to her bed and looks down at all her beautiful curly hair laying on the white pillow. The nurse is adjusting an IV when he picks up her hand and asks.

"Why are her hands icy?"

"Her body temp is not normal yet, and that's what we're working on right now: to get her temp up."

Michael sits on the side of the bed and picks up her hand to kiss her fingers while the tears streams down his face. Seeing her just lying there not moving is tearing him apart, but he is so happy she is still alive and he promises himself right at that moment he will never let her go because she is the love of his life.

Chapter Nine

She looks so lifeless and it's breaking his heart. All he can remember is Tamara laughing, playing, or saying something off the wall and crazy. She is too still and too quiet. He bends over to kiss her cool lips and her forehead like he has done for the past two years.

"Baby... wake up. Baby, please wake up, I love you. I love you so much and I promise I will never leave your side again. You're my best friend and the love of my life."

Michael is still in that same position with tears rolling down his face when everyone comes into the room to see her. Her parents rush to her side along with her brother. Adrienne and Thomas Walker are so thankful their daughter has survived, and her brother Joshua is holding her other hand with tears in his eyes.

Adrienne bends over to kiss her daughter and whisper in her ear in French. *"Je t aime (I love you)*. Please wake up baby, we need you, you are *Amour de ma vie." (love of my life)*

Thomas rubs his daughter's hair. "Your mother is right, sweetheart, you're the love of our lives and we need you to wake up to be our Tamara who we all know and love."

Joshua knows his sister is a fighter and knows she will be fine.

Just as he kisses her hand, Alexandra, Tamara's other best friend, bursts into the room.

Joshua looks up and sees her standing there with tears rolling down her face as he walks over to grab her to hold her.

"Baby, she's going to be okay."

"Joshua," Alexandra bit her bottom lip and holds on to him for dear life. "Joshua, is she going to make it? I just heard what happened and caught the first flight out here."

"Sweetheart, she's semiconscious, but not in a coma and she has acute hypothermia which means her body temperature is too low, but other than that, that's all they have found so far."

Alexandra lays her head on Joshua's broad shoulders while he rubs her back, and she holds him around his waist. The doctor comes back in to check her vital signs and tells everyone she is still stable, and she will not completely become conscious until later.

"You guys can go home to get some sleep because she will not know you're here. If anything changes, we will call you right away."

Everyone leaves except Michael. "I'm not leaving her. You guys can go back home, but I'm not leaving this hospital without her."

"Man, it's nothing you can do tonight, you might as well get some sleep." Matthew places a hand on his shoulder.

Michael chin up unblinking, focused eye contact with Matthew. "If this was my sister laying here, you can't tell me you would leave her."

Matthew nods his head. "You're right. There is nothing or no one who could make me leave this hospital. Do you need anything before we go?"

"No, I'm fine. I just want to be here with her." Michael sits there holding her hand.

His mom and sister come over to give him a kiss, along with Tamara's mother before they leave, and all the dads give him a pat on the back. Everyone has left out except Joshua and Alexandra. She was still holding on to him and not letting him go.

"Brother-in-law take care of my sister. Call me if there is any change and I'll see you first thing in the morning."

Michael looks at him with wide eyes. "I can't leave her, Josh. I love her too much to leave."

"I know. Try to get some sleep so when she comes to you won't pass out." Joshua and Alexandra leave out the door together.

When they get outside the room, Alexandra realizes she has nowhere to stay. "Joshua, I guess I need to find me a hotel room."

Joshua looks down from his towering height at the woman he has always bumped heads with. He grabs her chin for her to look up at him and stares into her sexy gray eyes. "Baby, you're going to stay at the Four Seasons, where we all are staying. I will make sure you get a room there and I'll call right now to take care of that. I don't want you worrying about anything."

Alexandra, who is a very independent woman because she has been on her own for so long with no family. For once she does not argue with him at all. She reaches up to caress his face. "Sweetheart, thanks for taking care of me because I can't think right now. I've never been so scared before in my life."

He grabs her hand as they walk out the hospital to join his family to get her a room at his hotel to make sure she is close to him while they go through this crisis. He knows from Tamara she is basically all alone, and he does not want her feeling that way because of what they are going through.

Alexandra has always known Joshua is too smart and a good person to act the way he does with women. Now she is seeing a different side of him which scares her because she has always considered him to be a jerk, but after this not anymore.

After everyone has left Tamara's room, Michael takes off his suit jacket and tie. He pulls the chair in the room up to Tamara's bed to be as close to her as possible. Laying his head on the side of the bed he holds her hand while praying he can hear her sexy voice calling his name again. Her hands are still freezing, and she still has not opened her eyes. He wants to see those hazel eyes.

"Baby, please come back to me. I need you in my life, I cannot live without you. I love you, Tamara."

He falls asleep holding her hand with his head laying on the side of her bed when about two in the morning, he hears his name softly.

"Michael...Michael."

He immediately wakes up and looks up to see a pair of hazel eyes looking at him. "Baby, I'm here. I'm here and I'm never leaving you again."

"Scared Michael...so, so scared."

"Darling, you never have to be scared again. I will take care of you. You're my world and I can't live without you."

"It's so cold...I'm so cold. Help me, Michael, help me. I...love you...love you."

"I love you, baby. I love you so much. I will never leave your side again. I love you, Tamara."

She smiles as she goes back out. He knows she knows he is there with her because her face has a peace on it that was not there before. They have a bond, and he knows with her in another world they are still bonding because nothing can keep them apart from each other. Michael goes back to sleep and sleeps until his family and Tamara's family returns in the morning.

His mother Katherine walks over to her son first. "Michael, honey, wake up. How is she doing?"

Michael looks up to see everyone there when he gives them a slight smile while he rubs the sleep out of his eyes. "She came to this morning about two. She called my name out and told me she's scared, and she was cold." He does not tell them how they tell each other they love each other.

"Thank God." Adrienne hugs him, because at least her baby has come to for a moment and she hopes it will lead to her waking up completely.

The doctor comes in and after saying good morning to everyone he asks them to please step outside, so he can examine her and check her chart. Michael still does not want to go; he will not let go of her hand.

The doctor smiles. "It's okay, young man. I promise she'll be okay and it won't take long, but I really must have you step outside."

"Come on Michael, you can stand right here by the door, but you have to let the doctor do his job." Christina pulls her big brother out of the room.

They all stand in the hall talking and trying to make Michael smile because he looks like hell. Just like his buddy James, he's always dressed and suave, but right now he looks like a train has hit him.

Michael walks over to the window to look out and his two friends join him. They always know when they need each other and have always been there for each other.

James puts his hand on his shoulder. "Talk to us, man. We can see and feel something is up."

"She also said to me she loves me, and she kept asking me to help her. I have never felt so helpless in my life. I do not know if that love is just as a friend or if she is in love with me. All I know is I am in love with her and want to spend the rest of my life with her. If it was left up to me, I would have the priest to marry us today. I'm so scared she's not feeling the same way."

Matthew the sane one out of them who is the most serious looks him dead in his eyes. "Michael, she was in love with you before this happened. Both of you were in love with each other and just did not know it. Why don't you play it by ear and let each day happen? Don't rush her as soon as she wakes up because she has been through a lot and in this case, you're going to have to take it slow and let her get back well first physically and mentally."

James, who talks foolish like Michael, being his usual self, comments. "No, you don't want to join our club of marriage. I can't believe that with the way you messed with me last year, you want to take the big step."

Michael smiles. "Man, I never thought I would want to marry anyone ever, but I want Tamara with me permanently and every day. I don't want to date her. I want her to be my wife."

"I heard that. You say the hell with the dating scene you're ready for the real thing." James chuckles at him.

"Hell yeah. We've been dating and not knowing it these past two years. After what just happened and almost losing her for good, I want to wake up with her every day and go to sleep with her every night." Michael has a gigantic smile for the first time in days.

All three men bump fists with each other, share a laugh just as the doctor comes out smiling and wants to talk to everyone.

"I have good news. Her body temperature is 98.6, which is back to normal, and she's awake and alert. We still have her on medication, but we have taken the intravenous fluids out of her vein and removed the nasogastric tube from her stomach. I will start her off with fluids only for a day, then she can eat some soft food. We still must monitor her to make sure she does not get pneumonia. Try not to get her too excited and I would suggest if she does not mention the plane crash, do not force her to talk about it. She will when she's ready. You can go back in now to see her. Michael, can I have a word with you before you go back in?"

Tamara's mom, dad, and brother go in first and then all her friends. The doctor and Michael go over to the corner to talk.

"I know you will not leave her side, so I wanted to talk to you because I know you're going to be the one who will be with her all the time."

"Yes, sir." Michael's heart races because he thinks he is going to tell him something bad.

"Her health is doing okay, and I don't see any problems there. Now it is her mental state I'm concerned about. She has gone through something so traumatic that most of us will never experience in a lifetime, so I want you to be there for her. You might have to take her to talk to someone for counseling or she might open up to you. Either way it goes after a period she will need to talk about it with someone. Just do not push her, but also don't let her never talk about it."

"I understand. I will make sure she is okay. We have always been able to talk to each other about anything and I know her better than anyone, so I will know when she is ready to talk. Thank you personally for saving her. I don't know what I would have done if I had lost her."

The doctor shakes his hand. "Good luck and I wish you the best. I know you two are going to live happily ever after. Just be there for her and have patience with her because she might shut down with you and it will not be personal. She just might be going through some emotional changes that might make her withdraw from everyone including you."

"I'm glad you told me because I'll have a head's up if she does. At least I'll understand why. I'm hoping because of the relationship we have always had, she will not shut down with me but if so, I'll know how to deal with it."

The doctor tells him to take care as he heads to another patient room and Michael goes into the room to see the woman; he loves more than his own life.

Chapter Ten

Tamara looks at the door and wonders where is he? She cannot believe he has left. Dianna notices she is uncomfortable and not paying any attention to anyone because she is staring at the door.

"Michael is talking to your doctor. He should be right in." Dianna moves closer to James as he gathers her in his arms just as the door opens.

Tamara's eyes light up when Michael walks into the room. He does not see anyone but her, and she does not see anyone but him. They stare at each other as he walks over to the bed. He bends over to kiss her and this time it is not a brief peck as they have always done in the past two years. He grabs her chin to tilt her face to his and gives her a long passionate kiss.

"How do you feel, baby?"

"I'm a little tired, but I feel better. Where were you?"

"I was talking to your doctor. Everything is fine," he sits on the bed to gather her in his arms. "Are you still cold, sweetheart?"

She shakes her head no to settle back into his arms. "I'm much better now you are here," she turns to look at him. "Please don't leave me, Michael."

Michael pulls her even closer to him. "Never baby. Never

again will I leave you."

They both close their eyes at the same time because they are so much in tune with each other. Dianna, Christina, and Alexandra sigh at the same time because they are looking at genuine love. Their friends have a love so deep for each other, all of them are in awe of it.

Joshua must break the mood because it is too much for him, so he says something crazy. "So, does this mean I should put you brother-in-law on my Christmas list, because it looks like you'll be at all of our family functions from now on?"

Alexandra smacks him on his arm. "Joshua, I swear something is wrong with you."

"What? I mean, I just need to know if he is going to be there for dinner when we exchange Christmas gifts. Because I was not planning on buying him anything, but I guess I better pick him something up, so he won't feel left out."

Everyone in the room laughs because they know that is something Michael would have said. It seems like Joshua fits right in with Michael and James. Love to talk foolishness.

"Joshua, only you would come up with something like that. Mommy and Daddy, I don't know where you got him from." Tamara laughs for the first time as well.

"Tamara, besides having friends in common. We also have in common two crazy brothers who are a mystery about where they came from. I see your brother is like my brother. Some things that come out of their mouths are plain out scary." Christina crinkles her eyes and nose holds Matthew while he rubs her back.

Just as they are discussing how crazy Michael and Joshua are, the door opens and in walks someone no one knows but Tamara. Francois Xavier Renaud IV from Paris, France has flown in to see Tamara when he hears she is on the flight that crashed into the ocean.

"Francois."

You cannot hear a pin drop because they do not know what Michael is going to do or say. With what he has been through, he is a walking time bomb.

"*Bonjour.* (hello) How are you? I caught the first flight out when I heard you were on that flight. I'm so glad you survived." Francois looks at the young man holding her, who he assumes is Michael.

"I'm fine." Tamara moves even closer to Michael. "Thank you for coming to see about me. As you can see, I have family and friends, and this is Michael."

Both men look each other up and down until Michael says calmly. "Francois, can I speak with you outside, please? Baby, I'll be right back." Michael bends down to give her a long lingering kiss to let Francois know she is his woman.

Tamara looks wide-eyed because she does not understand what is going on; all she knows is that her kisses with Michael differ from the past two years. He always would give her a peck on the lips, and now it is a genuine kiss. Right after Michael and Francois go out into the hall, Matthew and James go out there too. They want to make sure their boy is okay and if he needs them. They have his back.

"I'm going to say this to you one time and one time only. Leave Tamara alone. She is my woman, and I am going to make her my wife. If you had not argued with her and she did not call me crying at one in the morning, she would not have been on that flight. Yes, I told her to leave and come home to me. Now even though she almost lost her life, and thank God she did not, it also woke me up and made me realize that I love her, and not as a friend. I love her and I'm in love with her."

Michael comes closer to him to get right in his face and through gritting his teeth, tells him. "Stay the hell away from us. Do not call, email, text or contact her even through Facebook or Instagram ever again. If I ever see you on this side of the continent, I'll not be responsible for what I might do."

Francois purses his lips. "I knew there was something going on between you two. She talked about you too much, and the both of you were in each other's business and could not make a move without each other. Good luck."

He walks off and Matthew and James join Michael where he is

still standing. James was the first one who said something. "Damn Michael, you put that boy in check. You were not playing."

"Man, we have been through too much with our women. Matt, Chris pushed you away because of her business and James, your assistant kidnapped Dianna, and now this. I am stopping this right now because I do not want to go through anything else. In the past four years, we have had enough drama to last us a lifetime."

Matthew smiles. "You got that right, brother-in-law. I'm ready for all of us to be settled and enjoying our families with no more drama."

They all give each other high five and head back into Tamara's room like nothing happened.

"Is everything okay, baby?" Wide-eyed, Tamara wonders what Francois and Michael talked about.

"Everything is fine, honey. Francois said to take care, and he's gone back to France." Michael gets back in his same position on Tamara's bed to hold her in his arms.

"Well... that was really nice of him to fly all this way just to check on you to see how you were doing." Adrienne, Tamara's mother, said not knowing what really happened.

All the men smile because even the dads know Michael probably threatened his life to leave Tamara alone and to leave the city.

Joshua asks Michael seriously. "You handle that situation, man?"

Michael nods his head yes. Joshua nods back and both men know exactly what each other means. They do not have to say a word to each other to know Michael has straightened out the situation with Francois, and Joshua knows he will never see the Frenchman again.

Alexandra looks at Joshua, and he winks at her. She shakes her head at him because she picks up the male bonding that is going on and she knows why poor Francois has left for good.

"Joshua, what are you guys up to?"

"Nothing, baby. You know it's just a little male bonding. We're not doing anything wrong. I promise."

Alexandra, Christina, and Dianna say at the same time. "Hmm."

Tamara does not know what is going on; all she knows is that she is glad to be alive and with her family and friends, but especially glad she is back in Michael's arms. She is tired and closes her eyes while Michael holds onto her even tighter.

Dianna notices her friend looks tired. "Come on, all you macho men, let's get out of here to let them spend some time alone. Tamara, we'll be back later this evening."

Everyone goes over to give her a kiss and tell her to get some rest. Matthew, James, and Joshua give Michael a handshake and tell him if he needs anything to call them.

Joshua grabs Alexandra's hand, waggling his eyebrows. "Baby, let's go get something to eat and some drinks."

"Okay... let me get you out of here before you start some more trouble," Alexandra pulls him out the door.

"What!" Joshua laughs and puts his arm around Alexandra's waist. "You know life is exciting with me."

Alexandra raises her eyebrow and glances sideways at him. "That's the issue, it's too exciting."

Everyone has left, and the room is quiet with only Michael and Tamara there. Tamara turns her head with narrowed eyes and looks at him. "Are you going back to Memphis soon? Because I don't want you to leave me. I'm scared, Michael, and I do not want to be alone. I do not understand or really remember everything that has happened. I feel okay, but then again, I don't feel like my old self. I don't know if something is going on with my body or my mind is playing tricks on me because of what happened."

Michael sits up and hunches his shoulders. "Do I need to get the doctor...are you hurting anywhere? Baby, talk to me because I'm sure he's still here in the hospital or I can have him paged."

Tamara looks at him with shallow, rapid breathing. "I feel fine...I just feel like I'm in the dark about what the doctor found out about what might have happened to my body. He never went over the test results with me, so I'm scared."

Chapter Eleven

"What are you afraid of, baby?" Michael runs his knuckle down her cheek, then takes his hand to rub his fingers through her hair.

"I'm scared something is seriously wrong and no one will tell me. Michael, is there something wrong with me the doctor has told everyone else, and no one wants to tell me?"

"Baby, you know I have never lied to you, and I promise you they have found nothing wrong seriously. You had acute hypothermia because you were in the cold water too long and your body temperature was below what the body temperature normally is, but now your temperature is back to normal and you're going to be fine."

She let out a sigh of relief because she believes him. He has never lied to her, and she knows he would not start now. Just as they get comfortable, a nurse brings in a tray of food.

"The liquids are for you, Ms. Walker, and the food is for you, sir. Since I heard you have not left this hospital or floor to go get yourself something to eat, we want you to keep your strength up so you can take care of this pretty lady."

Michael smiles and shows his twin dimples. "Thank you.

Now that you mention it, I am hungry. I forgot I have not eaten in almost two days."

Tamara sips her liquids through a straw while Michael eats the burger and fries. After they finish eating, Michael turns on a movie for them to watch until Tamara falls asleep in his arms. He has dozed off too when the door opens and in walks Matthew. Michael gets off the bed without waking Tamara and gives her a kiss on her forehead.

"Is she okay?"

"Yeah, she fell asleep while we were watching a movie. What's up?"

Matthew has an overnight bag in his hand. "I brought you some toiletries with some sweats and tee shirts you can shower and change into. You probably want to get out of those suit pants. I'll sit here with her while you go in the bathroom to change, and I will take your suit back with me to have it cleaned. Also, there are some Gucci sneakers in there for you to wear while you're here at the hospital."

"Thanks, man. I hadn't realized I had not eaten until the nurse brought me in some food, and it would be nice to get out of these clothes I have had on now for two days."

Michael shower and changes in the bathroom, trimming his moustache and goatee, which has grown into a full beard. He feels like a fresh man when he comes out of the bathroom. Tamara is still sleeping, and Matthew tells him he is going home because his parents and Michael's parents are there along with James's parents enjoying the grandkids. He also tells him they will not be back at the hospital this evening since she is doing well.

"I'm sure her parents and her brother will be back. You know if you need us, though, call and we will be here."

"I know, man. Thanks for everything and give my nephew and niece a kiss for me."

Just as Matthew leaves out the door, Tamara wakes up in a panic because Michael is not beside her. "Michael, where are you?"

"I'm right here, baby." Michael walks back over to the bed.

"Matthew came back to bring me some fresh clothes. I showered while you were sleeping. You, okay?"

"I don't know why I get so scared when I can't see or feel you next to me. I just feel so alone." Tamara lay her head on his shoulder after he gets back into the bed with her.

"Baby, I will not leave you so you do not have to worry about being alone again. Where you go, I go. You want to watch another movie?"

Later that evening, Tamara's parents, her brother, and Alexandra come back to the hospital. They are glad to see Michael in some more clothes and he looks like he has gotten some rest. Tamara looks better and Michael is still laying on the bed with her, holding her in his arms. Her dad cannot be any happier his daughter has a young man who absolutely loves her. You can see it in his eyes, but he also knows it because he has let no one get close to her since all of this has happened, including him and her mother.

"How are you doing, pumpkin?" Thomas asks his only daughter after giving her a kiss on her forehead.

"I'm doing wonderful, Daddy. I don't want you and Mommy worrying, I'm going to be fine."

"We know you are. Has the doctor said how long you must stay in the hospital?" Her mother aggressively runs her hands through her hair, wanting to know how long it will be before her daughter can come home.

"Where are you going to go, sis, when you get out?" Joshua glances sideways with one raised eyebrow because if she wants to go to the beach, he will get his beach house ready for her in The Hamptons.

Tamara looks at Michael because she does not know when she can leave and where she wants to go when they discharge her. Michael has not thought about it because he is just glad that she is okay and knows they can go anywhere for her to recover.

"The doctor has not said to us yet when she can leave, and that's left up to Tamara where she wants to go to recoup."

Michael chins up because he does not care where they go, just as long as they are together.

They all talk some more, and Tamara's family leaves because they are going to dinner just as the nurse brings in Tamara's liquids and Michael's dinner. While they eat, they discuss her getting out of the hospital.

"Baby, when I get out, will I still see you?" Tamara tilts her head and stares at him because she wants him with her when they discharge her.

Michael pauses with his fork in mid-air and leans forward. "Sweetheart, wherever you go when they let you out of here, I'm going with you. If you go to New York, The Hamptons, Memphis, or stay here in L.A., I will stay with you. Wherever you go, they better have room for me because I meant what I said earlier...where you go, I go."

Tamara's smile can light up Times Square. "Really? What about work, don't you have to get back to your law firm?"

"Do you honestly think I would be any good at work while you were somewhere getting better, and I couldn't see for myself? I'm not thinking about work right now, the only thing on my mind is you. So, the answer to your question is no, I do not have to get back to work."

They watch movies and sleep off and on all night. It is a good thing she's not hooked up to any machines anymore because Michael is laying in the hospital bed with her, holding her close to him. The nurses come in to check on them occasionally and must smile at how peaceful they look laying in each other arms.

The doctor comes in the next morning at seven and after he examines her and read her charts, he has good news.

"How would you like to go home today, young lady?"

"Are you serious?"

"Yes. Everything looks wonderful and you can rest at home in a more comfortable bed than this hospital bed. You live here in L.A., don't you?"

Tamara shakes her head no. "I live in New York, I'm just out here in L.A. a lot because I'm a flight attendant and I fly out of L.A. frequently. Is that going to cause a problem?"

"Well…I can let you go, but I need you to stay here in L.A. for the next two weeks because you must come back so I can do a follow up and take x-rays to make sure you have not developed pneumonia. Will you have somewhere to stay?"

Michael jumps into the conversation, maintaining eye contact with the doctor. "That won't be a problem at all. My sister and our best friends live here in L.A., so we can stay with one of them or I can get a suite at any hotel in this city. When can she leave?"

"Well, in that case, I will write the discharge right now and as soon as they process it, you can go. I want her to eat soft foods for the rest of this week and she can start on regular foods next week. Also, bring her back in two weeks for a follow-up and if everything is okay, I will clear her to get back to work and with her life."

After he leaves, they must decide who they want to go stay with. Since there are two sets of parents at Christina and Mathew's house, they think it will be best if they stay with Dianna and James. Michael calls to tell Dianna the good news and ask if they can stay there with them. Dianna, happy she is going to be released, said she would get the downstairs guest room ready right now and to call her when they are ready because she will pick them up.

Chapter Twelve

After being released from the hospital, Michael calls the Walkers on their way to Dianna's house to let them know Tamara has left the hospital and to give them Dianna and James' address so they can come there to see her. He calls Christina and the other parents to let them know they have discharged her and that they are going to stay at James and Dianna's. The last call he makes is to his office.

"Lisa, I need to talk to you, so put whoever you're talking to on hold."

"Michael, where are you, and what in the world is going on? Amber came in yesterday looking for you and no one knew where you were, not even Bruce." Lisa bit her lip, happy to hear her boss' voice because she thought something had happened to him.

Michael goes into full details of what happened and tells her to rearrange his schedule because he does not know how long he'll be out and to transfer him to Bruce.

Bruce picks up immediately when Lisa tells him Michael is on the phone for him. "Man, where the hell are you and what's going on?"

Michael goes again into details about what has happened. "Bruce, I love her and I can't leave her side, so you're going to have to run the firm for me and if there are any major problems, call my dad or my Uncle Matt and they can help you out. Man, I'm sorry to put this on you, but I must stay with her until she's better."

"Michael, don't worry about the office, I got this. I'm just so glad she survived. I will take over your cases and reassign some to other people as well. Also, I will let Amber know what's going on since you walked out on her and no one had heard from you. I'll let her know you're okay and that Tamara survived the plane crash."

"Thanks, man. As soon as I straighten out my personal life, I'll be back to work."

By the time Tamara and Michael get to James and Dianna's house from the hospital, everyone is there waiting for them except Matthew and James, who are still at work, but they will be there as soon as they wrap up their day. Michael carries her into the house and lays her on the couch in the great room to see everyone. Tamara is so glad to be out of the hospital and to see Zachary and Kennedy. The kids do not understand why she is not picking them up but are thrilled Uncle Michael is throwing them up in the air like he always does. Katherine, Doris, Maxine, and Cathy ask her what type of soup she likes so they can cook up some dishes for her to eat. Katherine knows it is only a matter of time before she will be her daughter-in-law and wants to show her how much she loves her already.

"Sweetheart, I'm going to make all your favorite soups for you to eat the rest of this week and Michael, you make sure you fix her soft scrambled eggs for breakfast, and do not give her any toast or anything like that. Do you hear me talking to you?"

"Yes, Mother." Michael rolls his eyes while on the floor playing with his nephew and niece.

Katherine bends over to give Tamara a kiss on her forehead before she walks to go into the kitchen. Tamara bursts into tears. Michael immediately stops playing with the kids and rushes to her side while everyone stops in their tracks.

"Baby, what's wrong? Are you hurting anywhere? Do I need to take you back to the hospital?" Wide-eyed, Michael stops in his tracks also because he has never known her to just start crying out of the blue.

Shaking her head no with a shaky voice, she can hardly get out what is wrong. "I'm just so happy to be here with everyone and everyone is being so nice to me."

"Ah...baby, that's because we all love you and you are family. All of us here are family." Michael holds her in his arms as he kisses her face.

Doris, Matthew's mother, knows exactly what is wrong. "Michael, you need to take her to the guest room and let her take a nap. This is probably overwhelming to her with everything that has gone on and she just got out of the hospital. Honey, you go take a nap and when you get up, we'll have some soup ready for you to eat, but right now you need to get some rest."

Everyone nods while Michael picks her up to take her to the guest room for her to get some rest. When they leave, her parents thank them for taking care of their daughter.

"You guys have been wonderful to our daughter, and we don't know how we will ever repay you." Thomas' splayed fingers cover his eyes with one hand at how they have welcomed them.

Mike Sr. walks over to him to embrace him. "Just as Michael just said, you are family now. We love her and anyway, everybody knows they're going to marry so we really will be family."

"Everybody but them. You know those two will still swear they're just friends." Alexandra raises her eyebrows since she does not know if they have accepted their feelings for each other yet.

"I thought they married. I believe they are and just don't want to tell anyone." Joshua cracks up laughing.

Everyone laughs when Michael walks back into the room to ask what is so funny.

"That you two are married and have been. You just been keeping it a secret." Joshua sits down to cross his legs like he has said nothing.

"Hilarious, Joshua. No, we have not secretly married. We just have a close friendship, that's all."

"Oh lord, here he goes with the close friendship stuff. Give it a rest, brother-in-law. You two have never just been good friends. No man and woman who are good friends keep up with each other and know each other so well they can finish each other's sentences. Come on, you heard the doctor when she was out of it your name was the only name she called. I do not know a good friend who does that. Let it go man, please make my sister an honest woman."

Everyone turns around to look at Michael, but before he can say anything Tamara lets out a loud scream and he runs to the room to see what is wrong. All the ladies go until the guys stop them to let Michael take care of her.

"Baby, what is it? Baby, what's wrong?"

"Dark...it's so dark."

Michael climbs into the bed to hold her when he realizes she's having nightmares about what happened when she goes to sleep. While she was in the hospital, he was in the bed with her, so she slept comfortably without having nightmares. He knows now; he is going to have to stay in this room with her and they sleep together every night, so she can sleep.

"It's okay, baby. I will not leave you alone again, even to sleep. You want me to sleep in here with you?"

"Yes," her breathing has come back to a normal rate. "I don't think I can sleep without you. When I do not feel you next to me, I get scared, and it feels like I'm back in the water."

Michael holds her close to him while his heart is breaking. She is reliving what happened, but she does not want to talk about it yet. "Baby, whenever you need to take a nap, you just let me know and we'll nap together and when it's time for bed we'll come in here and go to bed together every night. You will feel me lying next to you from now on for the rest of your life. I promise you that."

He does not know if she just got it, but he just commits himself to her forever. And as soon as she gets the release from the doctor, he is going to ask her to marry him, so she will not have to sleep without him again. They both close their eyes to take a nap.

When they get up, James and Matthew are home from work, and she looks well rested and is hungry for the first time. As promised, the mothers have fixed dinner and fixed Tamara some chicken noodle soup, which she asked for. Tamara goes into the dining room to talk with the parents while Michael goes into the kitchen where Dianna, Christina, Joshua, and Alexandra ask him what happened this afternoon when she was screaming.

"I'm going to have to sleep in there with her. She is having nightmares about what happened. Even though she is not ready to talk about it. She just keeps saying it was so dark. As long as she can feel me next to her, she's not scared."

"She probably feels not so alone when you're there because when the plane crashed and she was in the water, she was all alone. Michael, you're going to have to stay with her until she feels secure again." Alexandra looks at Michael and tells him, because she knows some other people who have been in a plane crash.

"You're right, Alex. The doctor talked to me about that and told me to be there for her because health wise she is okay, but now there might be some mental changes she might go through. I don't care what I must do, I love her, and I'll do any and everything to make her happy again."

He walks out the kitchen before anyone can say a word. They all know he will do everything in his power to save his woman, to get her back on her feet. Michael knows how he feels, but they do not know if Tamara now knows how she feels. With what she is going through, they all decide not to put pressure on her about it. They also know it is going to work out and before the year is over with, they hope they will go to their wedding.

Sitting around the huge dining room table at James and Dianna's house, everyone is laughing and talking. The women fix a wonderful meal and Tamara is enjoying her homemade chicken noodle soup. Michael is glad to see her eating and smiling. Through-out the entire meal they keep looking at each other and Michael would wink at her, and she blows him a kiss. Everyone acts like nothing is happening because they are used to them interacting with each other. They just know now it is different because they are finally a couple. About nine they all are still at the table talking when Michael notices she is yawning and looks sleepy.

"Well, guys, excuse us, but my lady is getting sleepy, and I think she needs to go to bed."

Tamara reaches out to touch his arm because she is enjoying herself too much. "Honey, I'm fine. I don't want to go to bed yet."

He looks at her and can see she is tired. "Baby, you've been up all day, why don't we go watch a movie?"

She shakes her head in agreement and before she can say another word, Michael picks her up from the chair and takes her into the guest bedroom.

After everyone leaves and the dads are back at Christina and Matthew's house, they are outside on the deck talking.

"I think he needs to take her away somewhere when she's released from the doctor."

"You mean a getaway for just the two of them?"

"My son needs to be away from everything and everyone to express how he really feels so she can express to him how she feels."

"You're right. They need some serious alone time, but where should they go?"

"He should take her to his house in Key West where he goes to regroup, because it's secluded and the perfect place to start their lives together."

"You know what we have to do is plant the idea in his head."

Chapter Thirteen

B ack in James and Dianna's guest suite. Michael is a little
anxious about them sleeping together. This will be the
first time they have ever shared a bed together. In the
hospital the bed was so tight, and the nurses were coming in and
out throughout the night, but now they are downstairs in a suite
all alone. Michael has a pair of Ralph Lauren pajamas from James,
and he has the bottoms on, and she is wearing the top. When he
comes out of the bathroom from brushing his teeth, he stops,
because she takes his breath away. She looks so beautiful sitting
there in the bed with her curly hair tousle with only a pajama top
on waiting for him.

"What took you so long?" Tamara parts her lips slightly,
stretches her arms over her head, then runs her fingers through
her curly hair.

He smiles while showing his dimples when he joins her in the
bed. "Getting ready for you, baby. You missed me?"

"Yes," she moves closer to him while he turns on the TV for
them to watch a movie.

They say nothing else to each other and spend the rest of the
night cuddling and watching movies until they fall asleep. Tamara
sleeps through the entire night without waking up and when

Michael wakes up the next morning. She is laying halfway on top of him with her arms across his chest and her hair is everywhere. He smiles, because he knows this is how it will be for the rest of their lives when they wake up together. He pushes some hair from her face to kiss her forehead when she says to him with her eyes still closed.

"Good morning."

He whispers in her ear, a growl greeting because he still has sleep in him. "Good morning to you, beautiful."

She looks up at him, and he takes her breath away. This is the first time they have woken up together, even though they have shared a living space together off and on throughout the years. They always sleep in separate bedrooms and when they see each other, they both are up and dressed. He looks so masculine with a shadow of a beard and those light brown eyes heavy from sleep.

"How are you feeling this morning?" Michael rubs her back.

"I feel normal this morning. It is the first time I have felt like me since all of this has happened. I guess it's waking up in a fine man's arms. What woman wouldn't feel good?"

Michael chuckles. "Well... I don't know about fine, but I'm glad to know you're feeling good today. After breakfast maybe, we can take a walk around the property and play with the kids if you don't get too tired."

"I'd love to do that. Let us get up and start our day."

Michael showers first and slips on a pair of James chino shorts with a polo shirt then comes out of their suite to fix her some breakfast and talk with Dianna while Tamara is getting up to shower and dress.

"Hey Di, what's up? James gone to the office all ready?"

"Yeah. He said he had to be in court at ten and then he was through for the day so maybe you two could hangout, while Tamara and I spend some time together. How is she this morning?"

"Good. She seems more like herself this morning." He looks up when she joins them dressed in some black shorts, a white tee shirt, and some sandals borrowed from Dianna. She comes into the kitchen smiling and goes straight over to give Michael a hug. He stops fixing her breakfast to hold her while kissing her forehead, eyes, then a long kiss on the lips. Dianna lifts one of her eyebrows at the couple. She wonders what happened in the bedroom last night because they seem real cozy with each other. She cannot wait until James and Michael hang out, so they can have girl talk.

Tamara's parents call to say they will be over later, but Joshua and Alexandra are on their way over right now. Michael and Tamara are out taking a walk with Kennedy when James comes in and Joshua and Alexandra pull up right behind him.

"Where is my baby sister?" Joshua asks Dianna, smiles knowing his sister is okay.

"She and Michael took Kennedy for a walk, they should come back any minute now." Dianna kisses her husband because they still cannot keep their hands off each other.

Michael and Tamara walk back in, and Kennedy runs straight to her daddy because she did not know he was at home for him to pick her up.

"Hey baby girl. You glad to see your daddy?"

Two chubby hands grab his face because like mother, daughter must have all his attention. "Daddy...stay."

"Yes baby. Daddy is at home to stay." James kisses his little girl and hugs his wife at the same time while loosening his royal blue tie from his shirt collar. "Hey guys, you want to go shoot some pool. I'll call Matt to see if he can get away and Dianna, why don't you call Christina to tell her to come over so you girls can have some girl time?"

"That's a good idea and why don't we let the grandparents baby-sit at Chris's house, so the kids won't interrupt us." Dianna picks up her cell phone to get everything set-up.

Matthew comes by there to pick up Kennedy when he leaves his office to take her to his house, to change his clothes and to get Christina then they go back to James and Dianna's, so the guys can go shoot pool and bond while the women decide to watch girl flicks and talk. Michael holds Tamara in his arms because he does not want to let her go. This will be the first time they have been apart since the plane crash.

"Baby... are you sure you're going to be, okay?" Michael twists his lips while holding on to her real tight.

"Man, let that woman go. She will be fine. She is here with her girls. Be a man and step away from your woman for a minute." James laughs at his buddy because he's gone over this woman.

"I know that's right. You need to hang out with your boys for a while." Joshua laughs with James because they are two of kind fists pump each other.

"You know what?" Michael kisses Tamara all over her face while playing in her hair. "I'm not thinking about you two. I'm not ashamed to say I don't want to leave my baby."

"Michael, she's fine. I promise you we'll take care of her." Christina pulls Tamara out of her brother's arms.

James kisses his wife, Matthew kisses Christina and Michael pulls Tamara back into his arms to kiss her, but what surprises everyone is when Joshua bends over and gives Alexandra a peck on the lips as well.

Michael places his hands around her waist to hold her tight, squinting his eyes. "Baby, you are sure it's okay for me to go with these fools? Because I can stay here with you if you want me to."

"No sweetheart, it's okay, go with the guys. But are you going to be gone late?"

"Hell yeah. We might not get back until the wee hours of the morning." Joshua lifts his chin and replies before Michael can say a word.

Alexandra, who is standing right beside him, puts her hands on her hips and lifts her head. "Joshua Walker, you will not be out until the wee hours of the morning, you'll be back here in a decent hour."

"Yes, ma'am." Joshua drops his head because everyone laughs at him, including Michael and Tamara.

"I see your woman got you in check too." James throws back his head while they all go out the door.

After the guys leave, Dianna pours wine for everyone except

Tamara, she gives her some orange juice. They are ready for some serious girl talk.

"Okay, the first order of business is Alexandra. What's up with you and Joshua?" Dianna tilts her head and wonders if she missed another relationship that has developed.

Tamara's narrow eyes jump into the conversation. "I thought you two can't stand each other. It does not seem like that is happening now. Do I have a new sister-in-law, and everyone forgot to tell me?"

Alexandra sips on her wine, shrugs her shoulders. "Girls, I'm not lying. I do not know what the hell is going on. Tamara, you know me and your brother have been at each other from day one, but now—"

Dianna stops her and announces to everyone before they go any further, "Ladies, we must all agree whatever we talk about tonight does not go any further. We will not tell or repeat anything said to our men, not even in the bedroom."

"Okay Alex, do you like him?" Christina creases her brow, confused about what is going on with them.

"I don't know what I feel. I am so used to fighting with him but since all of this has happened, our entire relationship has changed. He booked me a room at the hotel and I did not have to do a thing. He made sure I ate and got some rest and has just taken care of me. I don't know if it's because of the situation we were going through that our relationship went in another direction. He felt the needed to take care of me, but now Tamara is okay. We probably will be back at each other again."

"Yeah, but can you go back to the way it was?" Dianna pours herself another glass of wine. "You two seem pretty comfortable with each other and he genuinely seems like he wants to take care of you, just like Michael is taking care of Tamara."

Everyone looks at Tamara and she knows it is her turn for them to ask her about her and Michael.

"You know we've been asking you for the past two years about you two, where do you stand now?" Dianna glanced sideways because she is all up in everyone's business.

Tamara pauses before answering because she knows this is truth night just between them. "All I know is our kisses are not the same as it used to be. He would peck me on the lips, but now his kisses make me go weak in the knees. I cannot sleep without him, but we still have not made love. I am afraid when he is not with me and right now, I am missing him when I know he is just with his boys, but I want him home with me. I don't know which way we're going, and I'm scared when I'm all well what will our relationship be then."

All the ladies are quiet because this is heavy even for them. They did not expect Tamara to open like this. She always plays it off about her and Michael's relationship, but tonight she is being very honest.

Dianna crinkles her nose, then downs the glass of wine and pours herself another one. "Lord have mercy. This is too much even for me. Alex, you do not know what is up with you and Joshua and for the first time Tamara you are not playing off there is nothing going on between you and Michael. Thank God, Chris, you, and Matt are doing fine because I would just pass out if I had to hear anything else."

On the other side of town, the guys are shooting pool and having a similar conversation. Michael asks Joshua what the deal is with him and Alexandra.

"I mean, come on brother-in-law; you cannot keep on saying you can't stand Alex, not the way you two have been acting with each other." Michael calls him brother-in-law for the first time.

Joshua, who they now know is just like James and Michael, always talk crazy. Like them, he takes nothing seriously but this time, he is profoundly serious.

"Guys, I'm going to keep it real. I don't know what the hell is going on. All I know is I want to take care and protect her, and I have never felt that way about any woman. I really can't stand her, so I don't know where those feelings are coming from."

Matthew bends over the pool table to shoot. "Here we go again. I have been through this with James and Michael swearing they're not involved and look at them now; one married and the other one might as well be married. Save us the trouble...admit to us and to yourself you like this woman."

James breaks the balls on the pool table, shakes his head and frowns. "You know he's right. Your sister and this nut here swore for two years they were just friends, and we all know no man and woman are friends the way they are."

"But that's just it. We have never pretended we were friends. We both have said and made it clear with each other we can't stand each other."

Michael, James, and Matthew look at him and smile when Michael says, "That's how it all starts. You're saying you don't like each other or you're just friends. That is the same song Dianna and James sang for fifteen years; they could not stand each other, but she was the one. You might as well accept it. Trust me, it will keep you from going through all the drama. Now let me call my baby, to see if she is okay. Hey baby... you okay... good I'll be home soon."

The guys talk some more, shoot pool and drink beer, and then they all go home to the women who control them. James, Matthew, and Michael know how they feel, but now their new friend, Joshua is lost and does not want to face how he feels about Alexandra. They know it is only a matter of time before everything will come out and he will be just as messed up about his woman as they are about theirs.

Chapter Fourteen

Monday morning, before Michael and Tamara start their day. As Tamara lies across the bed when Michael's cell phone beeps to let him know he has a text. She picks up the phone to give it to him when she looks down and sees a picture of a woman. As she walks into the bathroom to give him his phone before she can reach him, it rings just as the shower goes on.

"Michael, your phone is ringing." Tamara hollers out to him.

"Answer it for me, baby, and tell them I'll call them back."

Tamara hit the talk button but does not say hello because a female voice speaks to her first. "Did you get the picture?"

"Hello...who is this?" Tamara squints her eyes frowns.

"Who is this?"

"This is Tamara Walker, and whom am I speaking with?"

"This is Amber Anderson...and may I please speak to Michael?"

"You're the new attorney. Did you just send Michael a picture, and may I ask why?"

"So, you are the so-called friend who was in a plane crash and seems to have Michael at your beck and call. Yes, that was my picture, and I sent it to cheer him up since he makes me smile. I thought I could make him smile...so, may I please speak with him?"

Tamara's flush face removes the phone from her ear, not believing this woman is talking to her this way. "I'm sure he has made you smile because Michael likes to make people smile, but don't take it seriously because he's that way with everyone."

Before Amber can respond, Michael walks out the shower with a towel wrapped around his waist, stops dead in his tracks from the look on Tamara's face and before he can say anything, she throws his phone to him.

"Here is your little attorney on the phone who wants to make you smile...by the way, she's cute. Delightful picture she sent you." Tamara crinkles her nose as she storms out of the bathroom.

"What! Hello...oh hey, Amber. What can I do for you?"

"I just called to make sure you just got the picture I sent you and to make you smile. How are you?"

"First, how did you get my private cell phone number and if it's not about business, we have nothing to talk about. If you have any business issues, you need to take it up with Bruce since he's in charge of the office until I get back."

Michael hangs the phone up in Amber's face before she can say anything. He grabs a pair of shorts and a tee shirt to go find Tamara to explain what just happened because she does not look so happy with him right now. Dianna and James are talking in the kitchen when Tamara comes in slamming kitchen cabinet doors while she looks for a cereal bowl with her face scrunch up mutters something up under her breath. Michael comes into the kitchen with a furrowed brow and sweating.

"Baby, let me explain."

"Michael, I don't want to hear it. I am not your wife or girl-friend so you can see anyone you want to see, and they can send you naked pictures for all I care. Remember, I am just your friend. But I thought as your friend you would have at least told me you're seeing Amber."

"Baby, I swear I'm not seeing Amber. I don't even know how she got my cell phone number and what picture? She asked me if

I saw her picture...I do not know what everyone is talking about."

Dianna grabs her husband's arm to pull him out of the kitchen. "Let's go so they can have some privacy."

"Hell no. I want to see how all of this is going to turn out with them claiming they are just friends." James raises one eyebrow and stands at the kitchen sink eating a bowl of cereal.

"Dianna, you, and James don't have to leave...I'm leaving. Michael and I have nothing else to say to each other. What he does and who he does it with is none of my business."

Tamara runs out of the kitchen and leaves Michael, Dianna, and James standing there. Dianna picks up her orange juice. "I'll go talk to her, Michael. I suggest you stay here for a moment until she cools down."

"Damn man, you got some woman sending you naked pictures?"

Michael hunches his shoulders and massages his temples. "All I was doing was taking a shower and now I'm lost. I do not know what picture and I really do not know what just happened. Tamara told me my phone was ringing, and I told her to answer it and tell whoever it was I would call them back."

"Well, first you need to check your phone to see what picture she sent you and obviously, Tamara and Amber were on the phone with each other and must have had a conversation. I'm also gathering it didn't sit too well with Tamara."

Both men look at the picture and breathe in relief as is not a naked picture, but she is blowing him a kiss, which does not seem work related. James grabs the phone to look closer at the picture.

"She's cute. So, she likes you...please tell me you did not hit that. You know you should not be mixing business and pleasure."

"Man, I swear I have not hit that. We worked on a case in New Orleans together, and then I was having dinner with her in Memphis when I got the phone call about Tamara's plane crash. I rushed out to go to the airport and I have not seen or talked to her since. You know how I feel about Tamara. I'm not interested in Amber one bit."

"Oh, hell...I hope she don't turn out to be a stalker. You always end up with women who cannot leave you alone because you do not want them anymore, but they still want you and then they end up stalking you."

"Right now, I'm not thinking about that...what should I do to straighten out this situation with Tamara?"

"Let the professional of drama... my wife, tell you your next move. She's probably in there right now, all in your business and calming your woman down at the same time."

"Well...I guess I got my answer on how you feel about Michael because if you weren't in love with him, you would not be this mad. Did you talk to her on the phone, and what did she say?"

Tamara tells Dianna everything that happened, from her sending a picture to their phone conversation. Dianna listens and when she finishes, she simply says to Tamara, "She must not be someone he's talking to because he would not have told you to answer his phone. Michael is through playing around, Tamara. We saw him and how devastated he was when we didn't know if you were dead or alive. I saw him at the hospital with you; he has some serious feelings for you. Now, you two might not have really talked about your feelings yet, but he would not have you answering his phone if he were seriously messing around with someone else. Sounds like she has a crush on him but if you think about it, he really has not been around her enough to mess off with her."

Tamara calms down and realizes Dianna is right; his actions show he cares for her, and he has not left her side since all of this has happened. "You're right...he's been with me and has really stuck by me through all of this, but I'm not too sure about this Amber chick."

"Hey...I didn't say you didn't have to watch her because she might be out to get your man, but don't push him away. You want me to send him in now?"

"Yeah."

Dianna goes back into the kitchen where Michael is sitting and waiting. "Go in there and talk to your woman."

"Is she still mad, because I swear Dianna, I have not messed around with Amber."

"She knows that now. You two are okay."

Michael walks back into the bedroom suite they share and sees Tamara staring out the window.

"Sweetheart...I'm sorry. I did not know Amber would call me or send me a picture. I have not messed around with her and have no intention of having anything but a business relationship with her, I swear."

Tamara turns around, lips pressed together, knowing he is telling her the truth. She has been friends with Michael long enough to know he has never lied to her before, and she knows he is not about to start now.

"Michael, you bet not have picked up another stalker. I do not know why you always get women who cannot leave you alone. She was rude to me, and I think she might have done it on purpose."

"Baby, she is the least of our worries. Right now, we need to get you completely well so we can go on with our lives. You are my top priority and you always have been. Now come here and give me a hug and a kiss."

Tamara walks into his outstretched arms as he pulls her closer, then he bends down and gives her a long kiss.

"Our first fight." Michael laughs. "Damn girl, I would hate to make you really mad. You probably would hurt a brother."

Tamara smacks him on his ass and walks away, saying over her shoulder, "And don't you forget it."

Chapter Fifteen

The rest of the week, Tamara and Michael spend their time relaxing and enjoying each other and their families. They went shopping because Michael did not bring any clothes with him, and Tamara lost her clothes in the plane crash. A daily routine of breakfast then taking walks alone or sometimes with Kennedy is established.

One morning out on their walk, Michael wants to discuss the future. "Baby, do you want to keep flying or do you want to settle down somewhere?"

Tamara's mouth opens because she and Michael have not had a serious conversation about the future since their talk in New York at dinner. "I don't know what I want to do. I just know I want the doctor to say I'm okay, then I will take it from there."

Michael does not want to pressure her, so he changes the subject to talk about Joshua and Alexandra. "Baby, do you think they have something going on with each other?"

"Honey, I don't know. All I know is Joshua has been very attentive to her and I have never seen my brother treat any woman that way; as a matter of fact I have never seen Joshua with a woman. He keeps all his playmates to himself, but there is something different to how he treats Alex."

"They probably have feelings for each other and just do not want to face it. We'll just have to wait and see what's going to happen next with them."

Friday evening, they take Joshua and Alexandra to the airport to go back to New York. Both feel Tamara is back to herself and since she is going to the doctor next week, they feel they can return home.

While the men get their luggage out of the trunk of the car, Tamara and Alexandra have a chat.

"Girl... call me Friday to let me know what the doctor said."

Tamara hugs her. "Will do, and make sure you call me to let me know what's going on with you and my brother once you two get back in New York."

Alexandra crinkles her nose. "There is nothing going to happen between us because we were just comforting each other while we were going through what happened to you. You don't need to worry about me. You need to handle your business with Michael St. John."

Tamara smile. "That's the same thing Michael and I used to say, that we were close because of comforting each other last year after what happened to Dianna, so be careful with that. I'll call you when I leave the doctor Friday."

The following week before she goes to the doctor, Tamara and Michael go to the movies and out to dinner alone so Tamara can slowly start back interacting with people. Later in the week, they have dinner one night with all the parents. After dinner, while the women are watching TV and Tamara's parents have gone back to their hotel, the dads catch Michael alone to talk to him about taking Tamara away when the doctor releases her.

"Michael, when you take Tamara to the doctor Friday and if they release her, where is she going?"

"I don't know, Dad. We haven't talked about it yet."

Matt Sr. jumps in the conversation with steady eye contact with Michael. "Why don't you take her somewhere where you two can be alone?"

"Yeah. I think you should take her to your house in Key West.

It's secluded there and that way, she can rest while you and her talk to figure out which way you want to go with your relationship. Do you love her, Son?"

"Dad, I'm so much in love with her, I would go to the courthouse tomorrow to marry her. I love her just that much."

"Then you need to seal the deal. Take your woman away and let her know."

"Will do."

Michael walks off to go be with Tamara while the dads stand there giving each other high five.

"I don't know how we missed him and Tamara and thought he was going to hook up with Amber."

"I know, but we're back on track and once the doctor says she is good to go, I guess we can go back home and wait for the good news."

"I say we have done our job here."

"You got that right and since this is November, why don't we have a Valentine Day wedding this time?"

"I love that. That's the perfect day to get your son married on."

Friday is the day Tamara goes to the doctor for her two-week check-up. Her appointment is at one in the afternoon, so they have time to have lunch and talk. This is the perfect time for Michael to bring up taking her to Florida.

"Baby, I have a good idea. Why don't you let me take you to my house in Key West to recuperate? We can take walks, sleep, eat, and shop. You don't have to think about anything, and we can relax until all your strength is back."

Tamara put her fork down from eating her savory shrimp and scallops' fidgets. "How are we going to get there? Drive? Because I do not want to get on an airplane."

Michael is quiet for a moment; he steeples his fingers because he did not think about the fact that she might not be ready to fly again. "Sweetheart. You have got to get back on a plane and I think you know that. That's something you're going to have to figure out, also, if you want to keep flying for a career."

"Michael, I'm scared. I don't know if I can get on a plane yet."

"I know, baby. But I am going to be right there with you. That's the thing about wherever you want to go, I'll be right there with you. You know you cannot stay here in LA because it's not your home, and to get home, you will have to fly there. I just thought we could go to the Keys to be completely alone since you are not ready to be around many people asking you questions. Just think about where you want to go, and I'll be right there with you on the flight."

Tamara continues to eat and thinks he is right: wherever she goes, she is going to have to fly to get there. "Let's wait and see what the doctor has to say, and I'll tell you then where I want to go."

They finish their lunch and head to the hospital to see the doctor. Michael knows this news is going to change their lives forever. He does not care where they end up going. He knows it is time for him to confess his genuine feelings to her, and he hopes and prays she feels the same way. It does not surprise the doctor to see the couple with each other and after examining her and running x-rays, he takes the good-looking couple to his office to talk.

"Everything looks great. There is no sign of pneumonia and everything else is clear. Ms. Walker, you can get back to your regular life, including your sex life. If you feel tired, stop and rest because you have been through a lot. I would go to your personal physician in about six months. If you need your records from us, just call my office and we will be more than happy to forward your medical records to your personal physician."

He shakes the couples' hands and wishes them good luck with their lives. Tamara and Michael leave the hospital, grinning from ear to ear because even though neither one of them had said it out loud, they both were afraid the doctor had some bad news and now they both relieved she is fine.

When they get back to Dianna's house, she and Tamara's parents wait to hear what the doctor has said. When they tell them the good news, everyone hugs each other and her dad makes an announcement.

"Pumpkin, it's time your mother and I get back to New York. Are you coming back home so we can take care of you? And of course Michael, you are more than welcome to join us there." Thomas knows his future son-in-law will not let her go anywhere without him, so he might as well officially invite him.

Tamara drops her head because she knows she must decide on where she is going to go. She has put it out of her mind because she would have to get on another plane, and she is not ready to do that yet. Dianna looks at her and can read her mind; she jumps into the conversation.

"Tamara, you and Michael don't have to go anywhere. You both can stay here as long as you need and want to."

"Thanks, Dianna. Baby, what do you want to do?" Tamara aggressively runs her hands through her hair and turns to look at Michael for him to decide.

"I think, sweetie, you need to decide where you want to go. I don't care as long as I'm there with you. I don't care what city we're in." Michael pulls her into his arms and rubs her back.

Tamara thinks for a moment at what Michael had said earlier at lunch. If they go away, just the two of them, she will not have to talk to so many people and when she wants to be alone, she knows Michael will let her be alone and not force her to do anything, including talking. Right now, she also wants to be alone with him; she is not ready to sleep alone and not have him right by her side. She has decided.

"Michael and I are going to his house in Key West, Florida so I can think about my life. I have got to decide if I want to continue flying as a career. Right now, I still want to be alone, just not completely alone without Michael. We don't know anyone there, so I don't have to interact with any people."

Her dad comes over to take his daughter out of Michael's arms. "Baby girl, that's fine with us. We know Michael will take good care of you and going there might just be exactly what you need."

"Hey Tam, you feel like going shopping to get you some new beach clothes? You probably need some shorts, tees, and some bathing suits."

Tamara smiles because she stills love to shop and suggests her mother come along before they leave to go back to New York. Michael thinks it is a good idea and asks her if she needs anything, them reaches into his pocket for his Louis Vuitton wallet.

"Baby... do you need my American Express card to pick up some new clothes?"

"No honey, I'm fine. I can call my credit card company when I get to the store for them to charge everything over the phone."

Dianna snatches Michael's Black Amex card out of his hand. "Girl, you're crazy. If he wants to give you the Black Card, we can have some big-time fun. Don't you want to get another Hermes bag since yours was lost? Plus, you won't have to go through those changes with your credit card company."

Tamara's lip trembles as she thinks about the plane crash and how she has lost her Louis Vuitton luggage and her favorite orange Hermes Birkin bag. Michael notices the sadness that comes over her and it breaks his heart.

"Baby." Michael grabs her closer to him. "I don't care what that bag cost. I want you to go buy another one to replace the one you lost, and go to our favorite store, Louis Vuitton, to get some new luggage. Sweetheart, do not come back home without whatever you want."

"Boy, you must be in love because you're talking about some serious money." Dianna's eyes light up because she knows they are going to do some damage to his Black Card, and he does not even care.

This time, Tamara approaches him. She grabs his chin to bring him down to her level, and she gives him a kiss that makes him go weak in the knees. Michael would have given her every dime he has for her to respond to him that way.

"Thank you, baby. I don't know what I would do without you in my life."

"That's something you'll never find out because I'll be in your life for now and forever."

The women leave discussing what stores they are going to hit first while Michael takes this opportunity to talk to Tamara's dad.

"Mr. Walker, I love your daughter and I plan on marrying her. I don't want to rush her, but as soon as she is together physically and mentally, I'm going to ask her to marry me so I can take care of her for the rest of our lives."

"First, please call me dad, and welcome to the family. Second, I've seen with my own eyes how much you love my daughter and I know for a fact she could not have a better man to take care of her to spend the rest of her life with. I told the both of you there was something going on with you two." Thomas laughs at him because he refused to believe when they kept trying to tell him they were just friends.

Michael smiles and shakes his future father-in-law's hand. "Well, now you know she is not just my friend."

Thomas shakes his hand and smiles back. "I knew from day one. Adrienne kept saying maybe you two were simply good friends, but I told her no way. When you both were in the Hamptons last year with Joshua, he told us he saw more than friendship then, but he thought Tamara was playing one of her games. I know you know my daughter loves drama."

"Do I know? She and Dianna are the queens of drama, they love excitement. The funny thing is, I really did not know I was in love with her. I just thought she was one of my best friends."

Thomas places his hand on the young man's shoulder. "Michael, that's the best relationship to have with the woman you love. Adrienne and I met in Paris when I was there studying art and we were friends for three years before we started dating, and we have been married now for thirty-eight years. And let me tell you, there is nothing like a French woman to be angry at you. The woman has cussed me out so bad in French and even though sometimes I didn't understand what she was saying, I knew she was talking about me bad, but we could laugh about it afterwards because we were and still are the best of friends. Keep the friendship you have and you two will be fine."

"Thanks, sir. I plan to spend the rest of my life taking care of her and being her friend."

The two men go out on the deck to talk about their women and since one is completely French and the other one is half-French, they know they have romance, drama, and love to look forward to.

Chapter Sixteen

Once they boarded the American Airlines flight to Florida, Tamara would not let go of Michael's hand. She was hyperventilating and was so tense, Michael did not know what to do. Finally, he takes his other hand to rub her body in the hopes that it will make her relax. His warm fingertips going over her body ease some of the tension as he whispers sweet things in her ear to make her smile.

"Baby, everything is going to be okay. I promise you I will let nothing happen to you."

"I know Michael, I'm safe when I'm with you. I'm just still afraid, but not as afraid if I was without you."

She lay her head on his shoulder and finally lets his hand go when he pulls her close to him for them to get through the rest of their flight. By the time they touch down in Key West, she is more relaxed and remembers what she has always loved about being in the air. They get a rental car to drive to Michael's house, which is in a secluded area by the silvery blue and green Atlantic Ocean. Michael's house is a white house with a cozy porch and a pool surrounded by palms, fern, and royal poinciana trees. He has a terrace that is primarily used for outdoor entertaining. A table for eating under a covered dining pavilion looks at the ocean with draperies blocking out the wind and rain while you can lay or sit on white garden Pompeii furniture.

The colors inside the house were tans, caramels, and creams. The living room is a very indoor-outdoor space with a fireplace. Michael takes their bags up to his master bedroom and when he comes back downstairs, Tamara is laying on the couch with his iPod listening to Corinne Bailey Rae. Her eyes are closed. He pauses and tilts his head back with slightly parted lips and stands in the door, looks at the woman he has given his heart to. She looks so peaceful and content. He walks over to the couch, sits down, and raises her head for her to lay back into his lap.

"Baby... are you glad you made the choice to come here?"

She opens her eyes to meet light brown eyes. "Yes, this was the best thing to do. I do not have to be bothered with anyone. Am I really the first and only woman you have ever brought here?"

Laying his head back on the couch, he is going to open up to her about who he really is and not just the party person. "About four years ago, I was out in LA with James and we had been partying for days, and both of us were drained when James suggested we go to his house in Carmel, CA, his getaway for just him. When we got there and stayed for a couple of days, I slept probably twelve hours straight. When I woke up, I had never felt so rested. James was the one who turned me on to getting a place somewhere that was just for me.

I would come down to Florida, especially Miami, to party. I love Florida, so I bought some property here, but not in Miami, because that's where I party. This property here in Key West is to get away from everything and everyone. I brought no on here. You are the first woman I have ever brought here, and I have never shared this place with any family members."

"I feel so special you're sharing this place with me." Tamara smiles as she rubs his face.

"That's because you're special and have a special place in my heart no one else can ever have." Michael gazes down into those hazel eyes while he plays in her hair. "Let me get up to fix us a quick meal to eat on the terrace while we watch the sunset."

Michael goes into the kitchen to fix them a quick meal. While he fixes the meal, he remembers what Matthew said to him at the hospital to not rush her and take one day at a time. He is going to wait until the right opportunity to tell her how he really feels. They listen to Sade, Jill Scott and Corinne Bailey Rae while eating on the terrace to watch the sunset. After dinner, they cuddle up on one of the lounge chairs to share a bottle of wine and talk about work, traveling, and family. They lay there until eleven that night before they go into Michael's bedroom to go to sleep. They hold each other until they fall into a deep sleep and Tamara sleeps all night with no nightmares.

Since they left LA on Sunday and plan to spend the entire week in Key West. Monday morning, their routine starts with Tamara watching Michael take a swim the first thing in the morning in his pool, then they eat a light breakfast. After breakfast, they take a walk on the beach and play in the sand like two kids. When they finish their walk, they go back to the house to watch movies or read. After their afternoon nap, they get up to prepare dinner together to eat out on the terrace while sharing a different bottle of wine each night.

By Wednesday, they have their routine down pact, and it works well for them. Every night they hold each other until they fall asleep, and Tamara continues to sleep through the entire night. Thursday morning after returning from their walk on the beach, Michael goes out on the terrace to lie on the lounge chair to talk. He feels she is comfortable and relaxed enough to talk about what happened.

"Baby, it's time. It is time for you to talk to me. I need you to talk to me about what happened the night of the plane crash."

Tamara takes a deep breath and closes her eyes because she is still not ready to talk. "Michael, I'm not ready. I can't talk about it right now."

Michael sits on the edge of the lounger chair as he looks down at her to pull her up to be closer to him. "Baby, you know I have never led you wrong. I have never lied to you or asked you to do anything wrong. I care more for you than anyone in this world. If you want me to take you to a professional I will, but I know to move on you have to put this in the past. Please talk to me and we never have to talk about it again."

She lays back and closes her eyes while wrapping her arms around herself. "At first, I didn't realize the plane was having any problems. I have been flying so long little things do not bother me on a flight. One of the flight attendants knew who I was and came over to me and whisper the plane was in serious trouble and just as she said that it started losing altitude quickly and I automatically jumped into flight attendant mode. I started helping the passengers, then I grabbed a pillow and sat in the back with the crew. We then started going down real fast and I just started praying while holding on to the pillow for dear life. The plane broke loose in the water," she stops and pauses while the tears stream down her face.

"When I landed in the water, it was so cold and black. I kept saying prayers and I went under one time, then I came back up and saw a piece of a wing. I swam over and grabbed the wing, still holding on to the pillow."

Michael's heart is breaking, but he does not interrupt her because he wants her to get it out. "Don't stop, love. I'm right here, baby."

"My family, friends, and especially you were running through my mind... I would never see no one again. The next thing I know, someone was pulling me out of the water and wrapping me in blankets and when I woke up again, I was in the hospital." The tears run down her face in full force.

Michael bends over to kiss her face. He kisses each cheek and licks the tears off her face. A tear falls into her mouth and Michael sticks his tongue into her mouth to wipe the tear away. She moans when she feels his tongue in her mouth because this is a first for them. Her moan sends him over the edge, and he deepens his kiss with the full force of his tongue meeting hers. They kiss and kiss until both moan into each other's mouth.

He stops kissing her to suck on her bottom lip and then kisses her again, over and over. He stops again to look at her and her neck is an arch with quick breaths while her breast rises under her bathing suit. The look she has on her face, Michael will never forget stares at her beautiful body, he becomes instantly hard and reaches for her breast. Both cannot believe what is happening between them. They never have kissed each other the way they are now with him caressing her is so new to them both they are in another world. Michael stops and really looks at her because this is the first time he sees her as a woman. She is not his running buddy anymore, but a sexy woman who he wants to make love to.

"Tamara, baby, I want you." Michael leans forward with wide eyes. "I never thought you and I would get to this place, but now that we're here, it's no turning back for me. I could never see you again as just my best friend. When I thought I had lost you for good, I realized how much you meant to me."

Tamara reaches up to caress his face. "I didn't know I could feel the emotions I'm feeling right now either. You know once we cross this line it will change everything, and we can't go back."

"I know...but I don't want to go back to the way it was because I could never see you that way again. You mean much more to me than a friend. I want you and right now I must have you."

Chapter Seventeen

Michael caresses her breast through her bathing suit top as she rubs his chest because all he has on are some walking shorts and no shirt. Both breathe hard as he squeezes her breast at the same time his tongue is doing the dance of passion in her mouth. He cannot get enough of her and he does not want it to stop. She pulls back and looks up at him.

"Michael, what are we doing?"

"Tamara, I love you. I love you so much and I want you in my life and with me every day of our lives."

"Oh...Michael, are you sure, are you sure that's what you want?"

"Baby, I have never been surer of anything in my life." Michael takes off her top and her beautiful breasts spills out and he kisses and licks each one.

"Michael, it feels so good. It feels so good to be loved by you, please don't stop baby, please don't stop."

"Baby, I couldn't stop if someone put a gun to my head."

He must have her right now, right at this moment. He pulls her bottom down and looks at her laying there naked with a look she never thought she would see him give her. Her body is perfect with breasts that most women paid thousands of dollars for, small waist and abs that are a six-pack. He pulls down his bottoms and they are completely naked with each other.

She gasps because Michael has always looked good in his suits and casual clothes, but naked he is gorgeous. His body is perfect without an ounce of fat with a ripped six pack, and what hangs between his legs makes her body tingle just looking at it.

"Sweetheart, I have to have you right now." Michael raises her legs over his shoulders and enters her in one fast move, no foreplay. She screams out once he is inside of her.

"Michael, I love you...I love you."

"I love you too, baby, and I'm going to love you all day and all night. I did not know what love was until you. When I found you, it changed my entire world. Finding you has made me know what genuine love is and I plan to have this love for the rest of my life. Finding you has made my life complete."

Michael and Tamara make love fast and hard; it is if they both have built up sexual tension and now, they are releasing it. They climax together and call each other's name out at the same time, but Michael does not pull out because now he can take her slowly.

"I must have you again, baby. I want you and nothing has ever felt so good to me before. Tamara, you mean everything to me and I need to just be inside of you baby, so we can become one."

Tamara has tears falling down her face, but this time it is not from fear; it is from being loved the way this man is loving her. She cannot believe they have finally crossed that line. "I need to feel you close to me. Michael, when I thought I was going to die, you were the only person I kept thinking about and wanted to see."

"Oh...baby." Michael croons in her ear. "I died when they told me you were in a plane crash. I died right there on the spot when I thought I would never see you again."

Michael and Tamara both go over the edge with each other when they confess how they feel. They love each other so tenderly they both thought they were going to lose their minds. After climaxing over and over, Michael finally collapses on her, breathing hard, trying to get his heart rate back to normal.

He raises up to look at her smiles, shows those dimples she loves and gently pulls out of her. "Baby, let's get off this lounger and go into the house where I can love you right."

"Sweetheart, if you love me any righter, I'm going to lose my mind," she laughs when he pulls her up with him for them to go into his house.

Tamara, completely naked like him, stops in the kitchen to get something to drink. She grabs a glass and bends over the sink to get some water. Michael stands behind her and goes crazy just seeing her at his sink facing the ocean. He must have her again, right there.

"Baby, I have to have you right now." Michael has evidence that he wants her again she can feel his hardness against her ass. He bends her slightly at his sink and enters her from behind.

"Michael...baby, you feel so good." Tamara holds onto the sink while her lover works his magic on her by making love to her and caressing her breasts at the same time.

They stand there loving each other over and over until the climax is so powerful, they both just stand there with Tamara laying with her back against his chest as he kisses her up and down her neck.

Finally, he has the strength to move and asks her if she wants to go take a shower. She looks up at him, laughs. "You promise that's all we're going to do is take a shower?"

"Well...I'll try, but I'm not making any promises. I can't get enough of you, baby."

They go upstairs to the huge master bathroom to shower. Michael gets the water right for them to enjoy and washes his lady off. She washes him and just as she thinks they are going to make it out of the shower, Michael drops to his knees to lick her legs on up to her thighs until he finds what he is looking for. He sticks his tongue into her, and Tamara screams out because of what his tongue is doing and how erotic it is with the water dripping and falling off their bodies. He comes up to grab her mouth to kiss her where she can taste herself on his lips. She moans and in one swift movement, he lifts her off her feet so her eyes can meet his with her back up against the shower as he enters her, and she wraps her long legs around his waist.

They make love in the shower over and over from against the wall to him sliding down in the shower with her sitting on top of him riding him like a horse with her breast in his mouth and water falling off black curly hair. They love each other until the water turns cold and he gets them out of the shower to wrap them into two huge white fluffy towels. He dries her off and finally lays her in his bed where they have slept together every night, but now he is going to love her in his bed.

"Baby, I'm going to love you all night in my bed. Tamara, are you, my woman?"

"Yes, Michael, I'm your woman."

"Because I need to make it clear we are not just friends, we are lovers and I want the ultimate. I want to spend the rest of my life with you. When I told you at Dianna and James's house, you would never have to sleep without me, I meant it. We will sleep together the rest of our lives as husband and wife."

Before she can say anything, he enters her and like before she lost every train of thought once he was inside her. All she can think about is how good he feels and how good he is making her feel. His love making starts off slow and then it is as if he does not want to lose her, because he shows her through his love making.

By now the sun is going down. They started making love about one in the afternoon and now, it is about eight that night. They have made love off and on all day and are about to go into late night. Neither one seems like they do not want to slow down. They are all over each other in Michael's bed with the covers and pillows everywhere as he loves her. Then she would love him.

After one of their rounds, Michael is breathing hard. "Well... it looks like we have something else in common. I have never been this compatible with anyone in the bed before in my life. So, besides music, food, cars, and shopping, we both love to make love. When I say I can make love to you night and day, I mean it."

Tamara shakes her tousled curly hair. "I know, we have been making love off and on all day, and it scares me how compatible we really are."

"It's nothing to be afraid of baby, it is what it is."

Just as he says that, he climbs back on top of her and starts loving her again like they have never made love before. This goes on until they both pass out from exhaustion. This time when they fall asleep in each other's arms, it is not like all the times before. They fall asleep as a couple in love who want to spend the rest of their lives together. Just before they doze off, Michael whispers in her ear.

"I love you, baby."

She looks at the man who has now become her world. "I love you too, sweetheart."

The sun comes into the window and wakes Michael up and the first thing he realizes is Tamara is not in the bed with him. He listens for the shower and does not hear it, so he gets up to go downstairs because she is probably in the kitchen fixing them breakfast since they did not eat dinner because of all their love-making. When he walks into the kitchen and there is no trace of her in the kitchen, living room or out on the terrace, he runs back upstairs and her luggage is gone. He then goes back downstairs to go outside to see if the rental car is still there and it's gone. She has left him.

Chapter Eighteen

Michael stands there in shock. She had left when he was sleeping, but why? He packs, calls the airport to get a flight out, and calls a taxi to take him to the airport to go find his woman. The first place he heads to is L.A. because she probably has gone back to Dianna's. By the time he lands in L.A., he's exhausted from flying and making love all day and night with her. He gets in at twelve o'clock that night, goes straight to James and Dianna's and is beating on the door and ringing the doorbell at the same time. James opens the door with Dianna standing there right by his side.

"Oh hell, I know that look." James glances sideways at him. "Here we go. Do not tell me Tamara has disappeared. What is it with all our women that they like to disappear?"

"James, be quiet. Michael, what's wrong and where is Tamara?"

"She's not here? I just knew she came back here. Dianna, where is she?"

Dianna put her hands on her hips. "No, she is not here. Now what happened?"

Michael comes in and sits down on the couch in their great room. "She finally opened up to me about the night of the plane crash, and it led to us making love and confessing our genuine feelings to each other. She told me she loves me, and I told her I love her and want to make her my wife. We made love off and on for ten or twelve hours before passing out in the bed and when I woke up this morning she was gone."

"Damn boy, I didn't know you had it in you like that." James raises an eyebrow from those sexy bedroom eyes.

Dianna turns around to press her lips with a slight frown at her husband for him to be quiet. James looks back at her with a half-smile and shakes his head. "I'm just saying, he was all up in that."

"Dianna, please call her for me because if I call, she will know it's me even if I change my phone ID to show private, but if you call, she will just think you were just calling to see how she was doing."

"Yeah, but if I call her this late, she's probably not going to answer me because she is going to think you put me up to calling her. Crash here for the night and we'll call her in the morning."

Michael drops his head because he does not know if he can sleep, not talking to her and not knowing where she is.

James goes over to where his buddy is sitting. "Hey man, you know Dianna is right. For you to find out where she is, you need to listen to the pro. You know she knows about disappearing because she was the queen of disappearing. Get some sleep, I'm sure you need it, and we'll start fresh tomorrow."

Michael goes to sleep in the same room he and Tamara share and when he gets up about ten, the next morning James is there playing with Kennedy while Dianna is fixing breakfast. She stops because she knows he wants to find Tamara, so she picks up her cell phone to call her friend.

"Hey girl... how are you feeling? That's good. So, your flight down was okay, you didn't get scared——"

Before she can finish, Michael snatches the phone. "Baby, where are you, why did you run out? I love you baby, please don't do this."

"Michael, I had to leave. Everything was happening too fast.

With me almost losing my life and then you and me crossing the line of friendship and you talking about marriage, I had to get away so I can think."

"Baby, please tell me where you are, so I can see you and we can talk."

"I can't see you right now. I have got to figure some things out and I know I won't be able to do that with you around. Let me get myself together and then we can talk. Goodbye, Michael."

Michael stands there stares with wide eyes and holds Dianna's cell phone and all he keeps saying is, "She said goodbye. She said goodbye to me, it's over. She said goodbye."

James looks up from feeding his daughter cereal. "Michael, that's what people usually say when they hang up the phone from each other, they say goodbye."

"You don't understand. For as long as we have known each other, whether we are departing face to face or over the phone, we have never said goodbye to each other. We have always said 'talk to you when I talk to you.' For her to say goodbye, that must mean she plans to not talk to me again."

Dianna feels his pain because she has never heard them say goodbye to each other. "Exactly what did she say to you, Michael?"

Michael repeats back their conversation and Dianna thinks for a minute before she replies. "Michael, she needs some space right now. She has been through a lot and now after almost dying, she is now not best friends anymore with her best friend. You are in love with each other and have just faced it and you told her you want to marry her; she must take all this in. Give her some time. Tamara loves you, but now she must accept it herself before she can accept it from you so you two can move on. Remember Michael, the both of you insisted for the past two years that you were just friends and you have accepted your feelings about her before she has accepted her feelings. You had time to get used to it so now you must give her a chance to get used to it."

Before Michael can say a word, Kennedy flying down the hall

with her daddy's cell phone heads to the bathroom with Dianna running behind her trying to get the phone from her.

James smiles. "Kennedy likes to throw my cell phones in the toilet. I'm serious. This is the third phone she has flushed down the commode. They know me now at the phone store. But listen to Dianna, man, she is making sense you are going to have to give Tamara her space. She loves you, man."

Michael sits down on a bar stool at the kitchen island and feels defeated. He must listen to what they are saying and all he can do is wait until she is ready to talk and see him. Even though he is so worried about her being somewhere all alone and without him. He hopes she will take care of herself since he is not there to take care of her.

Dianna comes back into the room with Kennedy, laughing. "I was too late. Another phone down the toilet. James, why do you keep putting your phones where she can reach them? I think she thinks this is a game you're playing."

Kennedy claps her little chubby hands and giggles when James takes her out of her mother's arms. "Baby girl, you have got to stop throwing away daddy's cell phones. Look at Uncle Mikey, he's sad."

Kennedy's little head turns swiftly to look at her playmate, Uncle Michael. "Uncle...Mikey sad. Don't be sad," she says as she leaps out her daddy's arms into his.

Michael smiles for the first time that morning. "Yes, sweetheart, Uncle Mikey is sad because his other favorite girl has left him. But I still have you."

Dianna takes her daughter out of Michael's arms. "Michael, are you going to stay out here and wait for her to call?"

Michael takes his cell phone out of his pocket to make a call. "I don't know. I am going to make one more call to Joshua. Like you, Dianna, when you disappeared one time, you went home and none of us thought about looking for you there. If she went back to New York, Joshua would know."

Michael dials Joshua's office and waits until he comes on the line.

"Joshua." Michael fidgets, hoping and praying she is there. "Is Tamara there with you?"

Joshua frowns into the phone because he thought she was with him. "What do you mean is Tamara here with me? Mom told me the doctor had cleared her and that you and she had gone to your house in The Keys. What happens now?"

Michael tells him everything that happened, and he is back in L.A. because he thought she had come back there.

"You mean to tell me when you two finally tell each other how you really feel about each other and make love all day and night, she ran out. I do not believe my little sister. It took her forever to admit how she feels about you and now she is saying she does not want to talk about it. No, she is not here, and I have not talked to her since I left L.A. Let me see if I can find her. I'll call Mom to just check on her to see if she says anything about her being there and if she's not there, then I'll ask Mom for Alexandra's number and maybe she will know where she is, and I'll call you back."

"Thanks, man." Michael is now relieved that Joshua is in his corner.

"Hey man, we're family, plus you're my boy now." Joshua laughs because he cannot believe these two. "You two know you need to get it together and quit playing all these games. Just go on and get married and give me a niece or a nephew."

"Hey, that's what I'm trying to do. Your sister is the one who does not want to act right. I am ready to get married today if I could find her. Tamara is going to be the death of me, I don't know why everything with her must be so damn complicated."

Joshua laughs. "See, that's why I'm single. I don't have all these issues with any woman. I do not intend to marry, so I will not be worried about losing my wife. As soon as I find out something, I'll call you right back."

"Please call me as soon as you find out something and by the way you don't have to be married to lose your wife. It seems like with all of us we lose them before we marry them. Our women love to disappear."

Joshua shakes his head. "Hey man, that's why I don't get serious with anyone. With what you guys have been through, it will be a cold day in hell before I even think about settling down with one woman."

"Yeah, you're saying that now. Just wait until Alexandra takes you through something. Call me back."

"Alexandra will not take me through anything, because we're not involved with each other like that. I'll call you right back."

Chapter Nineteen

Joshua must be careful how he approaches their mother because he does not want to upset her with one of his sister's crazy stunts. At least she is completely back to her old self because this is something she would have pulled in the past. The only thing before it would have been for attention or a laugh, but this time it is probably because she's confused and scared about her life.

"*Bonjour. (hello)* How is Tamara doing? I haven't talked to her, and I don't want to call and interrupt her and Michael."

"*Bonjour. (hello)* Josh, as far as I know Tamara is doing well and still in Florida with Michael. I spoke to her Wednesday, and she said she was relaxing and enjoying her time there. Do you think they are going to get married?"

Joshua has his answer; she is not with their parents. "Who knows with your daughter? I know they love each other, but when they are going to marry, I have no clue. Do you have Alexandra's phone number, so I won't have to call Tam?"

Adrienne gives him Alexandra's cell phone number and tells him to call his sister and to come over to dinner tomorrow night and bring Alexandra. Joshua does not even ask his mother why she thinks he would want to bring Alexandra over for dinner when they have not spoken to each other since they flew back together from L.A. The only reason he is going to call her now is because he is looking for Tamara.

*"Au revoir." (goodbye) H*e leaves that alone to hang up to call Alexandra.

"Au revoir. (goodbye) A bientot. (see you soon)" Adrienne is glad to talk to her son about any situation.

Joshua dials and programs Alexandra's cell phone number into his phone. "Hey Alexandra, this is Joshua, by any chance is Tamara there with you?"

Alexandra drops her jaw after hearing Joshua's voice when she answers her phone. "No. I thought she was still in L.A. at Dianna's."

Joshua is quiet for a moment because he can hear the panic in her voice. "Baby, she's disappeared. She and Michael finally opened up to each other at his house in Key West, Florida, about how they feel about each other. They crossed the friendship line from what I hear all day and all night, until Michael woke up the next morning and she was gone. Now, no one knows where she is."

"Why do Tamara and Dianna have to have so much excitement going on in their lives? I have never known either of them to handle anything simple. They always must have some type of drama. I have not heard from her since I left L.A. I know Michael is about to lose his mind wondering where she is." Alexandra sits down in her chair, tries to think where she might be.

"Sweetheart, those two live for drama in their lives, but this time I think she has fears because of everything that has gone on. For the first time I am worried about her because of what she has been through. I don't want her to be alone. Baby, can you think of anywhere she might be?"

"Joshua, I do not know. That is the thing about being a flight attendant we can literally disappear anywhere in the world. She could be anywhere, sweetie. I don't know."

When she calls him sweetie in her sexy voice, it has Joshua to go weak at the knees. Alexandra rarely uses endearments with him, and it goes throughout him and before he knows it, he asks her out.

"Baby, would you have dinner with me tonight?"

Alexandra freezes for a moment before saying, "Why?"

"Why?" Joshua cannot believe this stubborn woman asks him why. When there are women who ask him out to dinner all the time. He must smile because she is so different from any woman he has ever dealt with. "Because I could use some company and I want to see you."

"I'm not buying that. If you want company, all you need to do is go through your phone and any woman you call would be more than happy to go out with you." Alexandra stands at her window, stares out with her hands in her dress pants pockets, dead serious because she cannot figure out where he is going with this.

"Alexandra do not make me come through this phone to strangle that beautiful neck of yours. I want to see you. I want to take you out to dinner, and I want to spend some time with you and only you. Will you please...go out to dinner with me?"

Alexandra's mouth is open at what he just said, all she can say. "Yes."

Joshua smiles. "Good. Now give me your address so I can pick you up at seven and here is my cell phone number and my private line number here at my office."

Michael's cell phone rings an hour later, and it is Joshua calling him back. He hopes he has some good news, and he will find out where Tamara is, so he can catch the next flight out to her.

"Man, I thought I was going to have to kill her before she would even go out to dinner with me."

Michael frowns. "Joshua, what the hell are you talking about?"

Joshua looks out his window. "I'm sorry, Michael, but Alexandra drives me crazy. I talk with mom, and she is not there, so I called Alexandra and she has not seen or heard from her. That's when I finally talked Alex into going out to dinner with me tonight. I think you should head back to Memphis and go back to work until Tamara surfaces. I promise you man if she calls me or even calls Alexandra, I will call you right away, but for now you got to wait it out my brother."

Michael closes his eyes because Joshua was his last hope of finding her. "I guess you're right, there's nothing I can do but wait for her to call me. Joshua, even if she won't tell you where she is, if you talk to her, please call me so I can know she's okay."

"I will, hey you know Tamara is just like Dianna they love drama just be patient and you'll have her back driving you crazy about something else." Joshua hangs up his phone to get out of his office early to go pickup Alexandra for their date.

As soon as Michael finishes talking to Joshua, Christina and Matthew walk in for them to have dinner with James and Dianna. One look at Michael and Matthew say the same thing James said when he sees his friend's face.

"She ran away, didn't she?" Matthew shakes his head because this was a pattern with their women. "I have never known women to run like the women we love. What happened?"

Michael tells them everything that happened while they were in Florida and the conversation he just had with Joshua and how Joshua suggests he might as well go back home to work and wait for her to call him.

Matthew wide-eyed and the first thing he says. "Damn man, you two made love for how many hours?"

"Matthew." Christina cannot believe that is all he got out of the conversation.

"What?" Matthew laughs, which is unusual for him because he is used to Michael and James stunts, but this even surprises him. "I'm just saying. Why would you wear the girl out like that, and she just went through everything she has gone through? No wonder she ran off."

James and Matthew bump fists with each other when Christina and Dianna both give their husband's dirty looks.

"James, you and Matt need to quit. Michael worried sick about Tamara. I know how messed up you two were when we left you two that I know you're not riding him with jokes." Dianna put her hands on her hips and stares at her husband and his best friend.

"Baby, come on, Michael knows we both got his back and we've been where he is, but you ladies need to stop the disappearing acts that seem to be a habit." James reaches out to grab his wife.

Matthew grabs Christina as well. "Sweetheart, even though you don't do drama like Tamara and Dianna, but you disappeared too. Michael, I agree with Joshua you might as well go back to work and wait until she shows up. That is what you two get for messing with flight attendants, you know they can go anywhere in the world. Come on man, join us for dinner and we'll drop you back off at the airport."

Michael smiles because his family and friends are right. Tamara can be anywhere in the world and will not show back until she is ready. He does not care how long it takes. He will wait until his baby comes back home to him.

Chapter Twenty

Joshua was nervous in his car that was driven by his driver to pick up Alexandra. He does not know what it is about her that drives him crazy, makes him angry, but he's also drawn to her. He has dated models and movie stars, but this one flight attendant has him nervous like this is his first date. He tells his driver he will be right back as he goes into her Tribeca penthouse in The Tribeca Zinc Building. He straightens his silk black and white tie that still looks crisp as he rings her doorbell, and when she opens the door, he holds his breath for a second. She looks beautiful, and he whispers under his breath. "*Tu es magnifique*!" (You are beautiful)

Alexandra has on a short royal blue dress which fits her like a glove. Her hair is curly and tousled, and her eyes look grayer than ever. He bends over to kiss her on each cheek.

"Good evening, sweetheart, you look wonderful."

Alexandra smiles and turns to lock her door when Joshua moans. Her complete back is out, and her back is flawless. He was not expecting this and it throws him off guard. This is going to be a long night. They ride in silence to Daniel, a French restaurant between Madison and Park Avenue where Joshua made dinner reservations. After being seated, he orders a bottle of 1982

Cheval-Blanc and orders their food in French fluently. When they bring the wine, Joshua makes a toast.

"Here's to many more dinners together and hopefully a wedding this year for my sister and Michael. Whenever they stop playing games and face the fact that they do love each other."

She touches her glass to his to break the ice between them. "Cheers and amen. I do not understand why Tamara and Dianna must make everything in their lives so complicated. Tamara knows she loves Michael, so why can't she just go on and have a relationship with the man and by the way... *parlez-vous francais?*" (do you speak french)

"*Oui.* (yes) Do you?"

"*Oui.* (yes) Fluently and I notice you ordered dinner fluently in French as well. I know your mom is French, did you learn from her?"

Joshua smiles. "Yes. Even though my dad is African American Cuban, mom insists we speak French. We would go to Paris every summer to visit my grandparents, uncles, aunts, and cousins. I grew up speaking French and English. We lived two different lifestyles because even though my mother has lived here for over thirty years, she is still very European and lives the lifestyle fully. I love French food, clothes and just the culture. Where did you learn to speak French?"

"We used to go to Europe every summer for vacation and we always stayed in Paris a month, and then we would travel around to other cities throughout Europe. I picked up the French language because I was there more than anywhere else. I also lived in Paris for two years after my parents died. I had to get away, so I stayed somewhere I love and spent my days visiting The Louvre Museum and The Pompidou Center for modern art, along with shopping. Tamara never speaks French around me, so I did not know you both grew up speaking the language."

Joshua grins. "Tamara never took to the language as I did. We speak it mostly when we are with each other, but it is a requirement when we are with our mother to speak it because she does not want us to lose it. Do you still have a house there now?"

"No, I never had a house there. I rented an apartment at the Saint-Germain that I loved because of the neighborhood where I could get to fashion boutiques, galleries, antique shops, and excellent restaurants. I did not buy a home there because I did not know where I wanted to live or what I even wanted to do with the rest of my life. Flying back home is when I decided I wanted to be a flight attendant, so I did not have to stay in one place. That's when I met Tamara and Dianna, and all the drama began."

"I can't believe how different you two are. My sister lives for drama and you seem to be the complete opposite of each other. How are you good friends with those two when you are so different? Dianna and Tamara are more like sisters who love to have something going on all the time...you don't seem to fit with them."

Alexandra throws her head back, laughs. "I balance them out. I am the sane one and believe me, those two needs someone sane around them. Growing up quickly because after losing both parents at the same time and no grandparents, I had to handle all my legal affairs and assets that were left to me by my parents and both sets of grandparents. I had houses to sell and art I had to decide what to do with and money to invest so I would have a secure future."

Joshua is quiet for a moment because he cannot think about life without his parents or his crazy sister. "You know if you ever need any advice concerning your finances, I'm here for you. That is what I do for a living and would make sure you're taken care of for the rest of your life. Now, I, understand why you have a maturity those two do not have. We all know Tamara and Dianna can pull some crazy stunts, and neither thinks they have done anything wrong."

Both shake with laughter while enjoying their dinner. They spend three hours in the restaurant talking, eating, and drinking wine. Joshua cannot believe how much he enjoys talking to her because she is so worldly and cultured. It is refreshing from all the women he usually dates, and he does not want the night to end. Alexandra shocked at how much she is enjoying Joshua's company. She knows he is a player, but tonight he is the perfect gentleman who is really concerned about her life. He even shares how much he likes his job and what he does when he has down time when it is just for him. She learns some new things about Joshua and has a new respect for him and how he looks at life. She now knows everything is just not a game to him. He has some actual reasons and purpose for his life.

On the way back to her penthouse in his car, Alexandra automatically cuddles up with him lays her head on his shoulder. He holds her close and realizes he does not want to let her go; he wishes it would take longer to get from the Upper East Side back to her penthouse in Lower Manhattan so she can stay in his arms. When they get back to her penthouse, he rides up in the elevator with her. He takes her key and opens the door. They stare at each other because they both see each other in a new light. Joshua for the first time does not know what to do. He does not want to cross any line that might offend her, but he does not just want to walk away, so he does something he has never done before.

"May I kiss you... goodnight?"

Alexandra smiles because she thinks it is cute. He feels uncomfortable. She knows this is a first for the ladies' man. "Yes, you may kiss me goodnight."

He gently pulls her into his arms and kisses her first on both cheeks, then his lips slowly meet hers as he kisses her gently on her lips. He steps back, looks into grey eyes, and she looks into hazel eyes and they both know they will never be the same with each other after tonight.

"Goodnight, baby. I will talk with you later."

"Goodnight, sweetheart."

Joshua closes his eyes when he gets back into his car, sitting there thinking about what just happened and how it has affected him. He calls Michael back to get his mind off Alexandra.

"Hey where are you now?"

Michael is at LAX waiting for his flight to be called. "At the airport to head back to Memphis, have you heard anything?"

Joshua massages his temples. "No, I have heard nothing. I just left from having dinner with Alexandra and she has me all out of sorts."

"Mmm." Michael smiles because it seems his future brother-in-law, he hopes, is confused about a woman. "So, you two are dating now?"

"Hell, man, I don't know what we're doing. I just know I have never enjoyed dinner with any woman as much as I enjoyed with her. I don't know, maybe I have been working too hard and just need to get out more and play around."

"Man, I don't know what to tell you because my life is completely screwed up. You know I am the wrong person to give out relationship advice. I swear man, those women are going to be the death of us before it's all over with."

Both men cannot do anything but laugh. One has a woman who has disappeared on him because he tells her he loves her and wants to marry her and the other one thinks he cannot stand her but cannot stop thinking about her.

Joshua's narrowed eyes looks out his car window. "I know, man. I'm glad you will be the one who's getting married whenever you find your woman."

They laugh again and said they will be in touch soon and tell each other to hang in there, things will get better. Once Joshua arrives home, he goes straight in and undresses, takes a hot shower, and goes to bed. He does not want to talk to anyone. Today has been a crazy day with Michael's phone call about his sister who is missing, and now dinner with Alexandra is just too much. He calls it a day so he can start new tomorrow. He hopes he will see things clearer tomorrow about Alexandra and hopefully, someone will have heard from his crazy sister so all of them can get on with their lives.

Michael boards his flight back to Memphis, hoping Tamara will call him to let him know she is okay. He must remember what the doctor said: she might shut down with everyone. He never thought she was going to do it with him, but he guesses with what all she has been through things got to be too much for her. Maybe he should have said nothing to her about marriage. Hopefully, that did not make her run, because he really wants to get married and soon. No long engagement because he almost lost her, and he is ready for them to live their lives together right now. All he can do is wait for her to contact him. No matter how long it takes, he will wait for her to call so they can plan the rest of their lives together.

Chapter Twenty-One

In Wilmington, North Carolina, Tamara is asleep even though it is twelve in the afternoon. She flew into Wilmington out of Florida because it was the first flight going out of Florida she could jump on. Her cell phone is off and not because she is sleeping, but it is off indefinitely. She is staying at a condo on the beach, so she can take walks to think. Her plans are to eat, sleep, read and rest. She does not want to talk to anyone, including family or any friends. She needs to think about her life. Now that she and Michael have crossed the line of friendship and have told each other they love each other, along with the way he made love to her like no other man has ever made love to her in her entire life, this is the time she must figure out what she is going to do about their relationship and if she wants to keep flying as a career. She knows she is in love with him, but she does not want to lose the friendship they have. She also knows she cannot and does not want to be without him. When she figures out everything that has happened in the past five weeks, she will go to him for them to talk about their future.

Meanwhile, back in Memphis. Michael is back at work and tries to act like everything is okay. Randall, one of his close friends there, knows something is wrong and takes his buddy out to lunch for them to talk.

"What's wrong, man? I know you and even though you are functioning normally, I can tell something is not right." Randall sips on a glass of water while he waits for Michael to talk to him. He leans back in the chair, takes off his suit jacket.

Michael stares out into space and knows he must tell Randall what is going on. "I love her, Randall, and I didn't know it until I almost lost her and now, I don't know where she is."

"I'm going to assume *her* is Tamara. What happened? And I want the complete story."

Michael tells him everything that has happened in the past five weeks and how his entire life has changed after he discovers how he feels about her. "The funny thing is I really thought of her as a friend because we never kissed or made love and I always thought to be in love, you had to make love. I did not realize the emotions and feelings I have for her are love and the purest love because it was without the sex, which means we truly love each other. Then when we crossed the line, she blew me away. We are like one in that area."

Randall does not know what to say because his friend is in love, and he knows he is in love for life. "Man, I told you there was something between you two everyone could see it from the outside because it was so powerful. We all knew you two were more than just friends. You don't have any idea where she is?"

"Not a clue. She could be anywhere in the world and I'm just going to wait. Now what has been going on in the office? How is Amber doing? Have the cases been given out correctly and is everyone on track with their caseload? I know I'll be here in Memphis for a while since I don't know where my woman is or how long she will be gone."

"Don't worry about the office Bruce has been on top of things, but you might need to talk to Amber. It quite upset her when you left her sitting in a restaurant not having a way home. That's how we found out about the plane crash because she was checking with everyone in the office the next day to see if you had called in to tell anyone what had happened."

Michael strokes his goatee. "I forgot about her that night and I'm so sorry I just walked off and left her sitting there. Maybe I'll take her to lunch to apologize to straighten things out with her."

Both men agree it will be the best thing to do and they finish their lunch, so they can get back to work. Michael has not seen Amber that morning, so he makes it a point to go by her office later in the afternoon to talk to her.

"Hey Amber, how are you?" Michael stands in her door before he goes in because he does not know how she is going to react to him.

"Michael." Amber comes from around her desk to give him a hug. "Are you okay? How is your friend Tamara?"

Michael lets out a sigh relief there is no drama with her, especially after the phone call she made when he was in L.A. with Tamara. "She's fine. She's blessed to be one of the few who survived. Amber... I'm sorry I left you sitting there in the restaurant, but when I got the phone call about the plane crash, I had to get there right away. I'm also sorry if I was short with you when you called me in L.A., but I was not expecting the call and I was still concerned about Tamara."

"I'm glad she made it. Is there anything you need me to do?"

"No, I'm good, maybe we can go to lunch one day this week."

Amber smiles. "I would definitely love to go to lunch."

Michael goes back to his office to bury himself in his work. He is working hard until later in the evening when his dad calls him on his cell phone to see how they are doing and to let him know everyone is back in Memphis. Michael tells him he is back at home also, and he will stop by later to let them know what is going on. Finishing his day about eight and before he heads downtown to his condo, he stops by his parent's house to tell them why he is back at home and not still in Florida, and that Tamara is missing.

Mike and Katherine sit there listening to their son while he fills them in on what is happening in his life. Mike Sr. cannot believe what he is hearing.

"So now you do not know where she is and no one else knows? I have never seen women who love to walk out on their men the way you guys' women do. They love to disappear." Mike Sr. laughs at his son.

"Mike, this is not funny. Your son is hurting and scared, but I must agree with you, Dianna, Tamara, and even our daughter Christina will walk out in a minute. Honey do not worry she will be back. She loves you too much, I could see it when we were around you two. You're just going to have to wait until she's ready to talk so you two can go on with your lives." Katherine gets up to kiss her son on the cheek then heads to bed because she and her shopping buddy, Doris, have a big shopping day planned for the next day.

"Your mother is right, she loves you and is probably somewhere getting her head together to accept her feelings for you."

Michael gets up to leave to go home, hoping Tamara has called and left him a message on his house phone even if she's still not ready to see him. He just wants to make sure she is okay.

Chapter Twenty-Two

Another week has passed and still no one has heard from Tamara. Amber now brings Michael breakfast and lunch and stops by his office all during the day. He is trying to be polite to her, and not discuss Tamara because he does not believe in discussing his personal life with his employees, but he feels she thinks something is going on between them. She keeps popping up in his office even when they have no business to discuss.

"Hey Michael, you want to grab some lunch?" Amber sticks her head in his door.

Michael does not want to mislead her. He shakes his head no. "I can't Amber, I'm tied up with some work."

"Okay, maybe we can get some dinner." Amber clasps her arms behind her body, waits for his response.

"Uh...I don't think so. I'm going home early to work from home and get some rest." Michael with a half-smile never looks up from what he is working on.

She leaves his office without making another comment. Maybe he is so upset about Tamara he is imagining things. Maybe she is just trying to be nice, and he is the one who sees more into it than it really is. He does not have time to deal with any woman tripping while Tamara is missing, and he is catching up with his work.

Michael works the rest of the week and the weekend to keep his mind off Tamara but decides the following Monday not to go into the office. He is going to work from home. This is the fourth week of not knowing where she is or talking to her. It is getting to him, and this is one day he does not want to see or deal with anyone.

He calls his office for them to have some files delivered to his home to work on and to talk to Lisa to let her know he will be back in the office sometime later in the week.

"Lisa, do I have anything important on my schedule I have to be in the office for today?"

Lisa looks over her calendar. "No, you do not have a court date today. It looks like you had plans to work in the office on files today to prepare for court at the end of the week. Michael, have you paid your personal bills for the month?"

"No. I've been so busy with my personal life, I forgot. Do me a favor and look in my desk drawer where I keep my personal checkbook, and go online to pay my bills for me, please. When you finish paying everything, put all my statements in my drawer. I forgot to ask you, did Bruce give you a raise?"

"Yes, thank you very much. Things are still tight, but better than it was."

"Here is a list of the files I need you to send downtown to me via messenger, and I'll see you in the office in a couple of days."

Michael has on his favorite black Nike sweats, no shirt, and no shoes when his doorbell rings, and he knows it is the delivery person dropping off the files he requests from Lisa when he opens the door and there stands Amber.

She looks him up and down. "Hey Michael, I brought the files you wanted. I had one file Lisa needed when she told me you were not coming in the office for some days. I told her there was no reason to call someone when I could drop them off myself. This is a nice condo."

Michael curls his lip, feeling uncomfortable dressed the way he is, but he was not expecting her to be at his door. "Thanks, but you didn't have to drop them off, we could have paid the delivery service."

"Not a problem. Do you want to go get some lunch? Or I could run out to get us something to eat?"

Michael frowns. "No thanks. Thanks for the files, but I must get back to work, I'll see you later in the week when I return to the office."

He escorts her to his door, grabs the files and tells her bye as he shuts the door in her face. He knows now it is not his imagination for her to drive all the way downtown to bring him some files, when they have a delivery service on call to deliver anything they want to be delivered. That is all he needs right now for some woman to be stalking him, especially who works for him, when his cell phone rings to break his train of thoughts.

"Hey Michael, I forgot to ask if you wanted to go to dinner or I can bring something back and we can have a quiet dinner there."

Michael hand grips his cell phone. "No Amber, I do not want to have dinner with you. I think we should keep our relationship on a business level."

"Okay, Michael, I'll call you tomorrow."

Michael closes his eyes as he leans against his door and states, "I cannot take this. I might have to leave town for a while to figure out how to handle this situation."

Meanwhile, Tamara has been in Wilmington now for the last few weeks and now she misses communicating with people. She knows she loves Michael and it is time she faces that for them to talk about where their relationship stands with each other after crossing the line of friendship, but not just yet. While taking a walk on the beach, she finally turns her cell phone on to listen to her messages. Everyone has called her except Michael. She smiles because he is respecting her wishes to leave her alone until she is ready to talk to him. Alexandra has called every day and Tamara feels she is ready to party, so she calls Alexandra, so they can hangout.

"Alexandra, what are you doing?" Tamara's tight-lipped smile calls to talk like nothing has been going on.

"Tamara, where the hell are you?" Alexandra stares with wide eyes and cannot believe she calls like they talked yesterday. "Everyone worried to death about you."

"I know, but I really had to get away by myself and not see or talk to anyone. But I'm ready to party, are you on or off?" Tamara asks if she is off work for seven days if she is flying for seven days.

"I'm off for seven, why?"

"Meet me in Atlanta, but you must promise me you will not tell Michael where I'm going to be. I am not ready to talk to him yet. Promise me Alex, you won't tell him, but I really need my friend right now so please meet me there."

Alexandra raises her eyebrows, pauses because she can hear in her voice. She needs her. "Okay, I'll meet you, but we're going to talk everything out and you're going to stop running and face this situation."

"Okay. I will book me a flight out right now, and let's meet at the Omni Hotel in Buckhead. Thanks Alex, I really need to see you to talk."

After Alexandra hangs up, she stands in the same spot because she does not know what to do. She promised she would not call Michael, but she did not promise she would not call Joshua. She and Joshua had gone to dinner, and she really had a good time with him. He was the perfect gentleman, not saying anything crazy or out of place. She must admit she is disappointed she has not heard from him since dinner, but she also realizes it was just dinner between friends and nothing more. Now she will call him, so he can tell her what to do and how to handle his sister. She dials his private number to his office.

"Joshua Walker."

"Joshua, it's Alexandra, do you have a minute to talk?"

"Hold on for one second." Joshua grins while he tells the people in his office, he must take this call and he will meet with them later.

"Alex baby, I'm glad you called. I have been out of town on

two business trips and just got back in late last night. I enjoyed dinner and cannot wait until we do it again. What's up?"

Alexandra smiles at least he has been out of town on business and maybe that is why he has not called her. "I just talked to your sister, and I don't know what to do."

"Baby, is she alright?"

"She's fine and wants me to meet her in Atlanta to hang out."

"Atlanta! What the hell is she doing in Atlanta and why is she not in Memphis talking to Michael? I swear, Tamara can do some of the craziest things and don't understand why she makes everyone's life as complicated as hers."

"I don't think she's in Atlanta now because she said she was going to get a flight out to Atlanta, so she's somewhere else she didn't tell me where. She made me promise not to tell Michael she was going to Atlanta, but she said she really needs to talk to me. Joshua, what should I do? I don't want to break my promise to her, and do you think I should go to Atlanta to see her, or should we just tell Michael where she is?"

Joshua aggressively runs his hand through his curly hair, closes his eyes for a second because his sister is going to be the death of him if she does not hurry and get her life together. "Sweetheart, I don't want you to break your promise to her. She sounds like she is still not ready to face things with Michael. Why don't you meet her in Atlanta, so she won't be there all alone?" Joshua stands up to look out his office window at the New York skyline. "That's why I have been so worried about her because she has not talked to anyone and has been all alone. Baby... call me when you get there after you see her, so I will know she is okay. Listen to her, then Alexandra, you are going to have to put your foot down and make her call or go see Michael. The man is about to lose his mind over her crazy butt. Do you think you can handle it, baby?"

"Yes." Alexandra shakes her head because her best friend is taking her through too much.

"Baby... are you sure? Because I'll catch a flight out with you right now if you can't handle this."

Alexandra lifts her head. "No Joshua, I'm fine. I'll call you when I'm alone, so she won't know that I called you to keep you posted on what's going on."

"Okay, I'll be waiting for your call, baby."

"Bye, sweetheart."

Chapter Twenty-Three

Once Tamara lands in Atlanta, GA, she feels human again and ready to interact with people. She knows she must talk to Michael but right now, she wants to unwind and let her hair down after everything that has happened. Atlanta is the perfect place to shop, eat, and party. Tamara checks into her hotel room then calls Alexandra to make sure she is still coming.

"Hey, where are you?"

"I just got off the plane and I'm getting into a taxi to come to the hotel now, so I should be there in a minute."

Alexandra checks in and calls Tamara for her room number, then goes straight to see her. "Girl, I have never been so glad to see you, let's go downstairs to get some dinner so we can talk."

The two beautiful women go downstairs to the hotel restaurant to eat dinner and to talk. Alexandra looks at her friend and must admit she looks good to have taken everyone through hell these past weeks.

"Okay, Tam, spit it out and I want the complete story to why in the hell you are not talking to that man?"

Tamara takes a deep breath before she discusses everything

that happened, from getting out of the hospital, staying with Dianna and everything that happened in Florida.

"Alex, I didn't know I could love or be loved the way Michael has loved me. He has been the perfect lover, friend, and confidant. Girl, we made love off and on I know for almost twelve hours. We started outside and then made love in every room, including the shower. I have never made love to anyone the way we did. Girl, that boy got it going on. He's some fire in the bed."

Alexandra sits there with her mouth wide open. "Tamara, the man is fine, got money, he's an attorney, and he loves you to death, so why are you sitting here with me and ran away from him for all these weeks?"

Tamara drops her head and bites her lip, then looks back up at her friend. "Alex, I'm scared. It's like it is too perfect. We were friends all this time and now I do not know what we are, and I do not want to lose our friendship. He even said something about us getting married and you know I have never thought about marrying anyone."

Alexandra massages her temples. "Tamara... grow up. You know you love this man, and it is obvious he loves you. I told you when he was in New York you two were in love with each other. I saw him with you when you were in the hospital, and you will never find another man to love you the way Michael St. John does. You cannot be forty years old, still running around partying and not committed to anything or anyone. Let me ask you a question. If Michael had been the one who was in a plane crash and you thought he had died, but he didn't, what would you want to do? Would you want to spend the rest of your life with him?"

Tamara freeze sits there stares out into space wide eyes, because she never put the shoe on the other foot. "Alex, if I thought I was going to lose him forever, I would want to die. I love him like I never thought I could love any man, and I guess I must accept it, so I can deal with this. When I was in the water, yes, I thought about all my family and friends, but Michael was the key person I thought about and was so scared and sad, I would never see him again."

"Well, that's your answer right there. He's your everything and now it's time to let him know it."

Tamara sips on her wine, smiles. "Yes, he is my everything and as soon as I get it together, I'm going to go to him to let him know."

Alexandra changes the subject because she does not want to put too much pressure on her. She knows her friend and sometimes when you want her to do one thing, she will do the exact opposite. They finish dinner and make plans to get up early to go shopping and sightseeing tomorrow.

As soon as Alexandra gets to her room, she calls Joshua as she promises him. "Hey, it's me, Alexandra."

"Baby." Joshua crinkles his eyes because he was waiting for her call for more than one reason. "Baby... are you in Atlanta and is Tamara there and is she okay?"

Alexandra relaxes when she hears his voice and realizes she likes the way he calls her baby. He just does not say baby, he sings the word. "Yes, I'm here and Tamara and I just had dinner and an exceptionally long talk. She admitted she loves him, and he is her everything. I told her to grow up to face that man and work things out with him."

"Good for you, sweetheart. Tamara needs to understand her actions are affecting other people as well. Not only has she taken Michael through hell, but all of us. Did she say she was going to call him or go to Memphis?"

"No. Hold on for a second while I take off my clothes."

Joshua almost drops the phone at what she just said. He does not know why, but his blood rushes to his head just thinking of her naked. He sits down because he has never thought of Alexandra in that way.

"I'm sorry Joshua, but I had those clothes on since this morning and I was ready to get out of them." Alexandra out of breath. "Now what were we saying?"

Joshua clears his throat before he responds because she sounds so sexy, he is trying to keep his composure "Uh... I was asking you if she was going to call or go see Michael."

"She didn't say she was, and she didn't say she was not. I dropped the conversation because we all know if you put too much pressure on Tamara to do one thing, she will do the opposite."

"That is excellent baby, you handled the situation right. What are you guys' plans for tomorrow?"

"We're going to have breakfast together, then go shopping all day and maybe do some sightseeing."

"Okay baby... are you going to call me tomorrow?" Joshua blushes, sounds humbler than he has with any other woman.

"Yes, I'll call you tomorrow night."

"Goodnight sweetheart, until tomorrow."

"Until tomorrow."

As soon as they hang up, Joshua calls Michael. He wants to tell him about his conversation with Alexandra.

"Hey man, you still up?"

"Yeah, I been at home all day. I worked from home because I did not want to see any people." Michael rubs his eyes from working all day and now is kick back laying on his couch watching the sports channel.

"I have some news. Alexandra is with Tamara."

Michael sits straight up. "Joshua, where is she? Do I need to catch a flight out right now?"

Joshua must think for a minute because he wants to inform Michael, but not cause problems between Alexandra and Tamara. "Okay, here's the deal. She made Alexandra promise not to let you know where she is, but Alex didn't promise her not to tell me and I didn't promise not to tell you what I know. I am going to keep it private where she is because right now, she still does not want you to know, but she is okay, and she told Alex she loves you and you are her everything. Alex told her to grow up and talk to you."

Michael lets out a deep breath. "Thank you, Joshua. At least I know she is okay, and she loves me. Why is your sister so crazy and stubborn?"

"Hey, man, that's your woman. I got my own issues with Alexandra Cunningham. I'm confused as hell about the woman."

Michael laughs. "Join the club my brother at least she has not disappeared on you like every one of our women have. Just keep me posted."

"I'm glad she's not my woman and would pull a disappearing act because I don't think I could go through that after hearing how messed up you are over my crazy sister."

Michael chuckles. "Hey man, I thought Matthew and James were pitiful when they had women problems and I used to laugh at them saying it would never be me...now look at me. I'm as messed up as they were when Dianna and Christina left them. Be glad you two are not together, so you will not have to go through all this drama. Let me know if you hear anything else."

Chapter Twenty-Four

Alexandra and Tamara are having a ball in Atlanta. They act like nothing has happened, and Tamara does not mention Michael's name again. Tamara also does not know every night before going to bed, her best friend is talking to her brother for two or three hours. Alexandra sums it up to herself she is just checking in with Joshua to give him an update on his sister, even though she looks forward to their conversations each night. They have been out shopping and to Martin Luther King Museum when they return to the hotel and Alexandra makes her nightly call.

"Hi sweetheart, how was your day?" Alexandra lays across her bed to talk to Joshua.

"Hey baby, it's going great now that I'm talking to you. How was your day? Did you buy me something?" Joshua throws his head back and jokes with her because he knows they have been out shopping all day.

"No, I did not buy you anything and I'm tired of shopping because today is Wednesday, and Tamara has not mentioned Michael. She has not talked to him or said anything about going to see him. Do you think I should bring it back up?"

"Yes, baby. Tamara will ignore things in her life and now is the

143

right time to tell her to get her butt to Memphis to talk to her man."

They talk some more on the strategy Alexandra needs to use to get Tamara to go talk to Michael, and then they discuss different things that are happening in their lives.

Joshua finally tells her. "Baby, I must go to Boston tomorrow morning for a meeting, but I'll be back in Manhattan by two and I have meetings for the rest of the day. Is it okay if I call you tomorrow night when I finish with my day?"

"Sure, if I don't answer just leave me a message because I might still be with Tamara, and I'll call you back."

"Okay, but if it's too late because sometimes my meeting will go on and on, I might not get out until late. I'll just try to catch you in the morning before you start your day. Talk to you soon, sweetheart."

"I'll talk with you later."

After shopping Thursday, they decide to go to The Cheesecake Factory for lunch. After they order wine to drink, Tamara must rush out to the lady's room because she needs to throw-up. Alexandra sits there in shock because she knows what is wrong.

"Girl, I don't know what's wrong with me, but I have been throwing up for the past three days. I must have some type of stomach bug." Tamara blows out her cheeks and asks the server to bring her a Sprite to drink.

"Tamara, did you and Michael use protection when you two were making wild passionate love?"

"No."

"Girlfriend, you're pregnant." Alexandra drowns down her glass of wine because this is too much.

"Oh, my God." Tamara puts her hands over her mouth and closes her eyes, not believing this is happening to her. "Alex... do you think I'm really pregnant?"

"Tamara. Be for real: if you two did not use any protection while having sex all day and all night, why you wouldn't be pregnant?"

"Let us get out of here. I got to go take a pregnancy test so I can decide what I am going to do. If I'm pregnant, I have got to straighten out my life with Michael and try to put our life back on the right track."

The ladies jump into their rental car and stop at the first drugstore to get a pregnancy test to take back to the hotel. They go straight to Tamara's room for her to take the test. Alexandra picks up a bottle of wine to drink because she now needs alcohol to deal with her friend's life. After five minutes, Tamara comes out the bathroom in complete shock.

"Alex, I'm pregnant. What am I going to do? Michael might not even want any children. How am I going to tell him he's going to be a father?"

By now Alexandra is drinking the wine right out of the bottle because this is too much. She almost died in a plane crash, crossed the line with her best friend, ran away from him, and now she is pregnant. Dianna and Tamara have always had drama in their lives, but this is just too much for anyone to deal with.

"You must go talk to him, Tamara. You can't keep this from him."

Tamara sits on the bed and cries because she does not know what to do. She has just accepted her feelings for him, now she must deal with this. "I'm going home. I need to see my family, go to my doctor to confirm this pregnancy, and then I'm going to catch a flight to Memphis to see Michael."

They call the airport to catch the next flight out back to New York, so Tamara can see her family and put her life in order. She knows she can no longer put off dealing with things in her life. She loves Michael and now she hopes and prays he loves her enough to start a family.

Meanwhile, in Memphis, Michael is back in his office working and dodging Amber. He's back at work after working at home for the last three days, and she has been by his office several times already. Lately, someone has been calling his phone at night who just holds the phone and does not say anything after he answers. He figures it is probably her. About one in the afternoon, Michael looks up and his dad and the two men he has always called Uncle

Matt and Uncle Charlie are standing at his door and they look profoundly serious. Too serious for Michael and he knows something is wrong.

"Dad, what's wrong? Has something happened to mom... or Aunt Doris or Aunt Maxine?"

"Son, I just got a call from the company's attorney and it's not a pleasant call. It's already in the newspaper, have you seen today's newspaper?"

"No."

"You must get your things because you have to leave immediately. Michael, you are being investigated for embezzling from the law firm. You must leave the property right now." Mike Sr. looks at his son and holds back the tears because he does not know if he can take this after everything he has been through.

"Are you kidding? Why in the world would I steal from my father?" Michael smacks his palm against his forehead, not believing how his life is going.

Matt Sr. comes around the desk to put his hand on his shoulder. "We know son, but until we clear this up and find out who has done this to you, you can't practice. We know you wouldn't do this, but someone has set you up to be the one stealing money from the law firm."

Charlie, a retired attorney too who had his own law practice in criminal law, is hurt Michael must go through this. "You got to give us the opportunity, son, to find out who did this."

Michael closes his eyes and slumps his shoulders because a person can only take so much. He gets up to pack his briefcase of his personal belongings because he knows he cannot take any files home, because he cannot work on anything until all of this straightened out. He tells his dad he will follow him to his house because right now, he does not want to be alone so he is going to stay in his old room for at least tonight.

Tamara and Alexandra are at Hartsfield Airport in Atlanta at American Airlines, waiting for them to call their flight back to New York. Tamara, sick from being pregnant, is eating crackers while drinking a Sprite. Both women are quiet because neither one wants to talk about what is going on. Tamara picks up the newspaper to read so she will not just be sitting there, thinking. She is reading when suddenly, she lets out a scream.

"Oh my God. I must go to Memphis right now. The paper said prominent Memphis attorney Michael St. John II is being investigated for embezzling money from his own father's law firm. Alex, I must go to him, I have to go right now."

She rushes up to the desk to show her badge to tell them she must get on the first flight out to Memphis because of a family emergency. They have a flight leaving at ten later in the night and they will put her on that one. Just as she comes back to tell Alexandra she is going to Memphis on the ten o'clock flight, they announce their flight to New York is ready to board.

"Tamara, do you want me to fly to Memphis with you, so you won't be alone?"

"No. You need to take your flight back to New York and I'll call you as soon as I talk with Michael, but I have to go to him because he needs me." Tamara hugs and gives her a kiss on the cheek and literally pushes her to catch her flight.

Chapter Twenty-Five

Alexandra arrives in New York at four that evening. She is so upset and confused about Michael and Tamara's situation she does not want to go home to be alone. She catches a taxi to go to Joshua's office to tell him what is going on. Fighting back tears, she tells the taxi driver to take her to Bank of New York on Wall Street and Broadway, where she hopes Joshua will not be in a meeting or gone for the day. She knows where his office is because she has gone by there with Tamara. The elevator takes her to the thirtieth floor and she goes straight to where Joshua's private office is asking his assistant if he is in.

"Hello, I need to see Joshua Walker if he's in."

Carolyn Jackson has been Joshua's personal assistant for six years and she has never seen this woman, or any woman, come to his office for him, because he keeps his private life with all his different women out of his business life.

"I'm sorry, but Mr. Walker is in a meeting and tied up for the rest of the day."

"Please let him know Alexandra Cunningham is here, and it's very important I see him?" Alexandra's droopy body feels like she is about to pass out.

"I'm sorry, Ms. Cunningham, but I cannot disturb him while

he's in his meeting."

Alexandra stares at the woman who will not go get Joshua, so she will wait. "I'll just wait for him. I'll take a seat over there until he comes out."

Carolyn does not know who this woman is and she hopes Joshua has not done something to her for her to be this determined to see him. This is a first for her to deal with a situation like this concerning her boss. Alexandra sits there for about two hours when Joshua finally comes out the conference room to give Carolyn something. He looks up and sees Alexandra sitting there and drops the file in his hand.

"Alex baby, what's wrong, what are you doing here?" Joshua gasps with his mouth wide open, not expecting to see her sitting there and not looking well.

Alexandra jumps up and grabs him by the waist. "Joshua, it's a mess."

Joshua rubs her back. "Baby, what is it and how long have you been waiting out here for me?"

Alexandra's lip tremble now and she has tears welling in her eyes; she looks into those same hazel eyes her best friend has. "I've been waiting for two hours. I'm so sorry, but I couldn't go home to be all alone and I didn't know where else to go. Everything is a mess with Tamara and Michael."

Joshua kisses her forehead. "You came to the right place, baby. I'll take care of you. Stay right here while I let them know I must leave."

Joshua goes over to his assistant, who witnessed everything said and done between her boss and the beautiful young woman and is in complete shock at how they interact with each other. He comes forward to her desk, fist clenched while his vein throbs in his forehead.

"Carolyn, if Alexandra Cunningham calls, emails, texts or comes into this office, I do not care what I'm doing or who I'm with, you get me. Never make her wait again for two hours or two minutes. Do I make myself clear?"

"Joshua, I'm so sorry I didn't know. I did not know she was

that important, or I never would have made her wait at all. I'm so sorry." Carolyn shrinks back because out of six years working for him, she has never seen or heard her boss angry.

"Just don't let it ever happen again. I am leaving for the rest of the day. Please cancel all my meetings because I have an emergency and I do not know how long I am going to be out. I will call you to let you know my status. Also call my car and tell them to come pick us up right away." Joshua walks back into the conference room to apologize and to let them know he must leave right away.

He walks back over to where Alexandra stands waiting for him and puts his suit coat jacket back on. "Let us go, baby. I'm going to take you home so you can tell me what's going on and I promise you I'll take care of you for the rest of the night."

Joshua and Alexandra leave his office and by the time they get downstairs his car is waiting for them, and they head to 5th Avenue to 325 Fifth Avenue where Joshua has a three-bedroom condo on the 40th floor with a 360-degree view of the city and river in one of the hippest and hottest spots to live in New York. Alexandra lays her head on his shoulder while he holds her close to him because she's upset and worried about Tamara.

When they get to his condo Joshua takes off his suit coat, tie and rolls his dress shirt sleeves up. He sits her in his lap and asks her to talk to him. She tells him Tamara is pregnant, and Michael is being investigated for embezzlement.

"What! I'm going to be an uncle and the baby daddy might go to jail."

"Joshua, this is too much. We were at lunch when Tamara throws up. She really did not know she was pregnant, so we left to go take a pregnancy test and that's when she found out. She was going to come back to New York to see her family and go to the doctor, then she said she was going to go to Memphis to see Michael. We were in the airport when Tamara read in the newspaper that Michael is being investigated for embezzling money from his own father's law firm. She jumps up and changes her flight to Memphis for a ten o'clock flight."

"Baby, this is too much. You left her in the airport?"

Alexandra slouches in Joshua's arms and lay her head on his shoulder. "Yes, she made me get on the flight before I could do anything else. What are we going to do, Joshua?"

Joshua picks her up to place her in the chair to get his cell phone to call his office. "Carolyn, I need you to get me a reservation for a flight out tomorrow morning to Memphis, Tenn. I need it for myself and Alexandra Cunningham. Call the car service after you book it and tell them to be here in plenty of time to get us to the airport. Call me right back with all the flight information." Joshua looks over at Alexandra and his heart is breaking because she looks drained. Before he can walk back over to her, Carolyn calls back to tell him they are flying out on Delta at ten tomorrow morning. He goes back over to Alexandra, and she has tears rolling down her cheeks when she looks up at him with huge gray eyes and it tears him apart.

"Baby, please don't cry. It is going to be all right. I know you scared, but I am here for you, and I just made flight reservations for us in the morning to go to Memphis to be with our friends. I know you want to be there and so do I."

Alexandra stands up and grabs him by his waist, holds on to him tight. "Joshua, I don't know how much more either of them can take. Tamara looked like she was about to break down any second. This is too much even for her."

"I know sweetheart. I'm worried about them both."

Alexandra stares up at him with tears still rolling down her face. He bends over to kiss the tears away and his lips find her lips. He kisses her and when she moans; he sticks his tongue into her mouth to meet her tongue. They kiss and kiss until he picks her up to carry her to his bedroom.

"Joshua, what are we doing?"

"I'm going to love you tonight, baby. I do not want you to think about anything. Let me love you tonight because I need this and so do you. Let go baby, let go."

Alexandra wraps her arms around his broad shoulders tighter because she does not understand what is happening, but she does not want to stop it. She must agree with him; she needs this. She needs him tonight. For the first time in her life, she is going to let go and not try to figure out what is going on between them. She has always been in complete control of her life since her parents died and do nothing without thinking it through to make sure it is what she wants to do until now...for the first time she is going for it without thinking about what she is about to do.

Joshua lays her in his huge king-size bed, never taking his eyes off her while he unbuttons his shirt and takes off his pants and underwear and stands there naked. He then bends over the bed to kiss her lips, eyelids, and nose.

He stops kissing her to slowly unbutton the white tailored shirt she has on and pulls her jeans down, then stands back to look at the sexy black bra and panties she is wearing. He then reaches behind her to unhook her bra as her beautiful huge breasts spill out. He takes each breast in his mouth one at a time and sucks them like lollipops. Then he kisses a trail down her stomach and, with his teeth, pulls her panties down.

"Alexandra...you are beautiful and sexy as hell and I'm going to love you all night long." Joshua looks at her with steady eye contact while reaching into his bedside table for condoms.

"Baby, I have never done this ever with anyone without being in a relationship with them. I do not do one-night stands, but I don't want you to stop... Joshua, make love to me...please, make love to me tonight."

Joshua parts his lips slightly and puts the condom on. "Baby, let go. Let go baby and let me love you tonight. We need each other and I promised you I would take care of you, and I'm going to take care of you for the rest of the night."

He enters her real slow and once he gets inside of her; he thought he was going to lose his mind. The woman he has claimed he cannot stand all these years makes him feel like no other woman has ever made him feel.

"Alexandra, you feel so good, I don't want to stop. Baby, I want you over and over. Being inside you feels like nothing I have ever felt before and I know I'm going to want you again and again."

"Sweetheart, I want you too. Don't stop baby, please don't stop."

They make love every way they can make love. She sits on top of him and holds his arms over his head while taking complete control of their lovemaking until he cannot stand it anymore and flips her on her back and tells her to wrap her legs around his waist. He pulls in and out of her over and over until Alexandra screams then she climaxes, which leads him to climax, and he screams out her name which is something he has never done with any woman before. About eleven that night, they decide to get up to take a shower together when Alexandra must ask him something.

"Joshua, what are we doing?"

Joshua washes her back. "Baby, for the first time in your life, don't ask questions. Let what is going to happen, happen. I would never hurt you and to be honest, I do not understand what is going on between us. All I know is right at this moment, it feels right, and it feels good. We are going to finish taking our shower and I am going to make love to you again and hold you in my arms for the rest of the night. Tomorrow, we're going to catch our flight to Memphis to help my sister and our friend."

This is the first time Alexandra does not try to figure out what he just said. She is so tired from everything that has been going on that she just shakes her head in agreement while reaching up to grab his chin to tilt to her, then she gives him a long kiss. "Take me back to your bed."

They go back into the bedroom and Joshua lay her on the bed and before joining her turns on his iPod with Corinne Bailey Rae playing softly in the background through the speakers in his bedroom. Dims the lights and joins her in the bed. He loves her from head to toe and kisses her lips and then trails his kisses all the way down her body until he is between her legs. He makes love to her there with his tongue as it goes in and out, then grabs her hips to get closer to her. His lovemaking with his tongue has Alexandra tossing and turning and shouting out his name.

When he comes up her body trailing her with kisses until he

reaches her lips where she can taste herself on him, Corinne Bailey Rae song '*Breathless*' is playing when he reaches for a condom to join her body with his just as she sings '*I get so breathless when you call my name, I often wonder if you feel the same*' Joshua feels he is going to lose it right then. Alexandra makes him feel things he has never felt with any woman he has ever been with. They make love over and over, and each time it gets better and better. Joshua takes her slowly again until Alexandra wraps her long legs around his waist, and he can feel her all the way to her womb, which takes him over the edge. It is as if he has become a madman who cannot get enough or close enough to her.

"Alexandra, what have you done to me? I can't stop. I want you again and again. Baby, you feel so good." He arches his neck and takes quick breaths as he looks into those gray eyes.

"Joshua, I never thought you and I would be here like this. Sweetheart, you make me feel things I have never felt before either."

Exhausted, they hold each other to get some sleep but cannot keep their hands off each other. Their lovemaking starts early that evening and now it is late night, and they still are making love to each other.

"Baby, I know you are tired, but I can't get enough of you."

"Yes." Alexandra lays in his bed and rubs his chest. "I have never been this way with anyone. You would think with what I have been through today with your sister, I would be ready to pass out, but I still want you as well."

"That's because of all this good loving we're sharing. Baby, you are taking me to another world, a world I have never been in with anyone else." Joshua grabs her chin to raise her head so he can look into those gray eyes that drive him crazy.

He leans over to give her one of the most tender kisses she has ever had in her life. They both close their eyes at the same time because they realize no matter what has gone on in the past between them, there is a passion they have for each other that is so strong, neither one can deny it.

Chapter Twenty-Six

Back in Memphis, that same night, Michael sits in his folk's great room in shock, how much more is his life going to fall apart. He still has not talked to Tamara and does not know when he is going to hear from her, and now his career has fallen apart. His dad is trying to comfort him, to let him know it is going to be all right.

"Michael, we're going to figure out who is doing this and why they are setting you up. Son, I know it seems your world is falling apart, but I promise you it will be okay."

"Dad, why is all of this happening to me? Why is it the one woman I finally fall in love with runs away and now someone is trying to ruin my career?"

Mike Sr. looks at his son because right now, he cannot do anything to help him; all he can do is to be by his side to help him get through this.

"Michael, it's time for you to call your boys. Call Matthew and James to let them know what's going on, because you know they would want to be here with you."

Michael makes a fist because he knows he needs to talk to them, so he dials Matthew's cell phone.

"Matt, this is Michael."

155

"Michael, what's wrong?" Matthew knows something has happened from Michael's voice.

"Matthew, I need you and James, someone has framed me for embezzling funds from the law firm. Matt my entire life has fallen apart."

Matthew let out a deep breath. "What! I'll call James and we will get the family together out here and catch the first flight out. Hold on buddy, we will be there tomorrow, and I promise you we will find out who did this to you, and we will find your woman. We have stayed out of that, but now it is time for us to find her. We'll see you tomorrow."

Michael tells his dad what Matthew said and he goes home to sleep in his own bed. Mike Sr. tells him as soon as they get in, all of them will come downtown to his condo so they can put their heads together to figure out who is doing this. Driving home, Michael is worn out. All of this has taken a toll on him. He goes in, takes a shower, and falls into his bed and goes to sleep. Suddenly, he can feel someone in the room with him and when he looks up, there is Tamara. Taking off her cashmere gray sweats and underwear, now completely naked, she gets into the bed. She scoots closer to him to spoon with him when Michael growls in her ear.

"Where the hell have you been?"

"Wilmington, North Carolina, and Atlanta... by the way, I'm pregnant, we're going to have a baby." Tamara passes out from exhaustion.

"WHAT! Tamara, we're going to have a baby?" He sits straight up, pumping his fist in the air.

Michael smiles and pulls her closer to him, then falls back asleep to sleep some of the most peaceful sleep he has had in weeks. Not only does he have his baby back, but they are going to have a baby. A baby they created out of their love and now maybe, one part of his life is coming back together.

The sun comes through Michael's floor-to-ceiling windows in his enormous master suite when he opens his eyes to see Tamara laying halfway on top of him with her curly hair everywhere and her arms across his broad chest. Michael moves some of her hair back and rubs her back; she moans and that is all he needs. He flips her over on her back and gets on top of her and with one quick move, he is inside of her.

"Baby, please never leave me again. Baby, I love you so much and I cannot live without you. You're my everything and my life is not complete without you in it. I love you, Tamara."

Tamara opens her eyes to look into his light brown eyes she loves. "Michael, I'm so sorry I ran away. I was scared and confused. I love you so much because when I found you, I found my everything. Finding you has changed my life. Please, just love me now because I have missed you so much. I need you, baby."

Michael slows his pace with her because he wants it to last longer. "Baby, I've missed you too, and I was so worried about you. Do not take me through that again, ever."

Michael pulls out and throws her legs over his shoulders, then he enters her again and moves as if he is riding a horse. Then he pulls out and turns her onto her stomach so he can enter her from behind. He kisses up and down her neck while Tamara screams out his name over and over. He stops to lie on his back then sits her on top of him. She holds her head back. They rock back and forth together until they have the ultimate climax at the same time and yell out together. "I love you."

Out of breath, Tamara lies on Michael's chest while he caresses her back and shoulders. He cannot believe she is back, and he will not let her go.

"Sweetheart... are we really going to have a baby?"

Tamara raises up to look at him. "You always said I was your baby mama. Well, guess what, it's true. Michael, we're going to have a baby, how do you feel about that?"

"You have made me the happiest man in the world. Tamara, I love you and the thought of something inside of you we created out of our love. I'm thrilled and overjoyed. I can't wait to be a father and a husband."

"I'm so happy to hear that because I want this baby so much and I want to be your wife, but we have this minor problem: you might go to jail. Baby, what the hell is going on?" Tamara gets up off him for them to talk because this is something serious.

"How did you find out?"

"I was in the airport in Atlanta leaving to go to New York on a two o'clock flight when reading the newspaper and saw the article. Immediately, I changed my flight and could not get out until a ten o'clock flight that night. I knew you needed me with you... there was no way I would not be here for you."

"Thank you, baby. I do not know what is going on. My dad, Uncle Matt, and Uncle Charlie came to the office and told me I had to leave because I was being investigated for embezzling money from the law firm. Why would I steal money when I make a good living and I wouldn't steal from my family?" Michael tilts his head back, closes his eyes because even though Tamara is back. He still has this major problem about his career.

"Baby, what are we going to do? I cannot bring our child to jail to see their father. I cannot believe our lives. I almost die in a plane crash. We have been separated from each other for weeks. I'm pregnant and you about to go to jail for embezzlement."

"And I have a woman stalking me."

Tamara sits straight up. "Michael, what woman is stalking you? Okay, this is just too much. I told you about messing around with all those crazy women you used to mess with and now some woman doesn't want to leave you alone."

Michael gathers her back down to him to hold her in his arms. "Baby, I swear it's not a woman I just met or from the past. You will not believe who it is? Amber at work keeps calling me at work and home. She popped up here to bring me files when I was working from home because I didn't want to see anyone, and I keep telling her I do not want to go to lunch or dinner with her and she keeps showing up with food and asking me to go out with her. Plus, someone has been calling me at home and just holding the phone. I believe it's her."

"Okay, I'm not too far along to kick her ass for messing with my man. I told you when we were in L.A., at Dianna and James when she called and sent you a photo, she was going to stalk you."

Michael laughs. "Chill out, tiger. You will kick no one ass in your condition. If anything, happens to you or my child, I will not be going to jail for embezzlement, but for murder. We're going to leave her alone. I'm sure when she sees us together, she will get the message and remember I can always fire her once I straighten out this mess and get back to running the office."

Just as he said that his doorbell rings. He looks at the clock by his bed; he knows his family has made it in. "Baby, that's everyone including our L.A. family to figure out who is doing this to me and how we can catch them. You can join us downstairs whenever you feel like it."

Michael gives her a kiss and grabs his shorts and tee shirt off the chair. He runs down the stairs to answer the door to see his family. In walk his two best friends, his sister Christina, Dianna, his dad ,and his Uncle Matt and Uncle Charlie. Christina immediately goes over to hug her brother and then steps back so he can be with his friends. Their bond cannot break and they have been there for each other through everything. James, who usually has something crazy to say, is serious and worried about him.

"Man, how are you doing? Don't worry. We'll figure this out, we've been through much worse and survived so we'll survive this."

Matthew strokes the nape of his neck and agrees with James. "We both have almost lost our women and Christina lost her business and you thought you had lost Tamara in a plane crash, but we got through all of that... we'll get through this."

Michael stares wide-eyed at his friends from childhood. "Man, I didn't think my life could get any worst. I know I like to hangout and party, but you both know I love what I do and I would do nothing wrong to lose my license. And you know I would never steal money, especially from my father's law firm."

All three men agree and stand there bonding when down the stairs comes Tamara in one of Michael's dress shirts and a pair of shorts and says, "Baby, do we have any orange juice?"

"Yes baby, there is some on the top shelf."

159

Chapter Twenty-Seven

Everyone stands there with their mouths wide open. Matthew and James cross their arms when Matthew asks, "So, she's back. Where has she been and what's going on now?"

Michael grins and shows his famous dimples. "Well... she was in Wilmington, North Carolina and Atlanta, Ga., she's pregnant, and I'm about to go to jail."

Tamara hollers out from the kitchen. "And he has a woman stalking him."

Mike Sr. shakes his head. "Lord, have mercury. Why is it when you guys fall in love, it is always drama? Why can't you fall in love, get married, and have babies? No, I swear each one of you has had something going on. Matthew, Christina pushes you away because of her business that her best friend and right-hand person stole from her while setting it up to make it be someone else, and James after fifteen years you and Dianna play cat and mouse games by disappearing with each other until Dianna disappeared for real when kidnapped by your assistant, and now Michael you two take the cake. First, you swear for two years that you're just friends, then Tamara almost died in a plane crash, when you finally tell each other how you really feel she disappears for weeks, now someone is setting you up to go to jail, she's pregnant and you have a woman stalking you. I am glad we have no more sons to get married because I am too old for this. I just want a simple fall in love, get married and give me some grandchildren."

All the kids stand there looking at him like he has lost his mind when Tamara comes back in the room with windows facing the famous Mississippi River and laughs. "Now you know that would be dull for us. We live and love drama."

Matt Sr. presses his lips with a slight frown, rolls his eyes, and agrees with his partner in crime. "Yes, but you guys live and love too much drama. This is just too much. Now that we have one issue solved of Tamara being back, we must figure out how to keep your baby daddy out of jail."

Just as Matt Sr. says that, Michael's doorbell rings and everyone freezes because with them, they are afraid to answer the door because trouble seems to follow them wherever they go, especially when all of them are together. Michael opens his door and there stands Joshua and Alexandra.

"Joshua, Alex, what are you guys doing here?" Michael hugs Alexandra and gives Joshua a manly embrace.

Tamara flies to her older brother's arms, then hugs her other best friend. Joshua picks her up to swing her around, puts her down, and whispers in her ear. "Tamara Gisselle Walker. I could strangle you for putting all of us through this hell."

"Now Joshua Stephane Walker, you don't mean that, especially since you're going to be Uncle Joshua." Tamara steps back with her hands on her hips. "Alexandra, your man is threatening to kill me and that's just plain not nice; bedsides, my baby daddy might not like that."

"I know that's right. Even though she drives me and everyone else crazy. I can't live without her, so please don't kill my baby mama." Michael pleads with Joshua, because this has always been a joke between them.

Alexandra lays her head against Joshua's shoulder while he holds onto her tightly. "I swear, you two really need to grow-up. I feel sorry for that poor kid having you two for parents."

Everyone in the room laughs because Michael and Tamara are still the same, just as carefree even though, they are going to be parents. Joshua cracks on Tamara and Michael as they high five each other.

"Husband and wife and mother and father, I don't know what the world is coming to with you two being actual adults."

James waggles his eyebrows and jumps in on the fun. "I know that's right, but they held out as long as they could. It's just scary you two are going to marry and have a family."

Michael stops laughing because he realizes he has not made it official between him and Tamara, so he goes over to where she is now standing between Dianna and his sister, Christina, to get on one knee and grabs her hand.

"Tamara Walker, I love you with every breath that I have in me, and I want to spend the rest of my life with you. I want to be there with you to help raise our beautiful baby together, to grow old together and take my last breath in your arms. Will you marry me? Will you become my wife?"

Everyone in the room is quiet and moved by his honesty and sincere words. They know Michael as the crazy one out of everyone, but he just displayed how much heart he really has. Tamara stands there with tears running down her face and gets down on her knees to be at the same level he is.

"Michael, I've been running from relationships all my life and now I don't know if I could live my life if I didn't have you in my life. You and this baby I carry are the most important thing in the world to me and yes. I will marry you and spend the rest of my life with you."

All the women are crying now when Michael and Tamara kiss as if they are the only ones in the room. The dads are so proud, and his two best friends and his new best friend and future brother-in-law are touched as well. They know his playing days are over.

"Man, I guess you can hand over your cell phone now with all your women's' numbers because your days of playing around are over." Joshua cracks on Michael before saying something serious.

"All jokes set aside. Welcome to my family. My sister could not have picked a better man. I'm proud to be a part of your family and I know you three have been friends forever and have a bond. I just hope all of you can think of me as a genuine friend and one of your brothers now."

Michael, James, and Matthew surround Joshua with the manly hug they have always done with each other, and all their women know Joshua is a part of their private clique. He has become one of them. The dads know they have another adopted son and are proud to have him a part of their family. Mike Sr. goes over to his future daughter-in-law to give her a hug and welcome her to the family.

"We couldn't be prouder to having you a part of our family. Thank you for loving my son and giving me another grandchild, and Joshua, you are now one of our sons and we couldn't be prouder to have a fine young man like you in our family." Mike Sr. hugs Tamara then goes over to Alexandra. "Young lady, you are also now our daughter. I want you to always feel Matt, Charlie, and I are here for you and whatever you need or want, we will always be here for you."

Mike Sr. hugs her, and Matt Sr. and Charlie join him while Alexandra is really crying now because she does not have an immediate family of her own. She only has one aunt and uncle, and a cousin, Jason, who she is close to, but he is always busy because he is an architect and real estate developer.

"I don't know what to say. Tamara, you and Dianna both have been like sisters to me and now to have this extended family, I'm just overwhelmed." She burst into tears when Joshua immediately goes over to comfort her.

"Don't cry baby, please don't cry. You know I'm here for you and I'll let nothing happen to you. Now you're a part of our family and all of us are here for you." Joshua brings her closer to him, closes his eyes, holds her tight, because he knows from a previous conversation with his sister and the conversation they had when they went to dinner that she is all alone in the world.

Michael raises an eyebrow because this is a different side of his future brother-in-law that he has never seen. What has been going on between these two he does not know about?

Dianna and Tamara both go over to hug their friend because she does not break down about her life too often and they hate the fact she is all alone. Dianna usually says crazy things, but this time she is dead serious.

"Alex, you're like a sister to me and Tamara and now it's official we're your family and will always be here for you."

Michael's doorbell rings again and in comes Katherine, Michael and Christina's mother, Matthew's mother Doris, James's mother Maxine, and Dianna's mother, Cathy carries in his nephew and niece who both knocked out.

Chapter Twenty-Eight

"Mother, why are these kids knocked out for life? What have they been doing?" Michael grabs Kennedy while James grabs Zachary and neither kid moves.

Dianna and Christina bump fists with each other while both cracks up laughing because they knew this was going to happen. All the men stop and look at them like they are crazy.

Christina goes over to kiss her son on his chubby cheek. "We knew if they took our kids with them while they shop, it would knock these two out the rest of today and probably tomorrow. We all know no one can hang with the serial shoppers and live to talk about it."

Katherine looks her daughter up and down. "I do not know what you are talking about. Our grandkids absolutely love spending the day shopping with us. You should see all the cute things we got them."

Doris jumps in to bag up her best friend and shopping buddy up. "When we saw they were getting tired after the third mall, we brought them home."

Mike Sr. fixes his gaze at his wife and her shopping buddies. "You took these kids to three malls? Poor things, they might not wake up for the rest of this week. Katherine, I cannot believe you have had these kids out shopping since ten o'clock this morning and it's now six o'clock."

"I don't know what you're talking about. They just got tired after we left the last mall and passed out in the car. Before that, they were having a ball in every store we went into. I think they took after their grandmothers; they have a natural thing for shopping. What's been going on here?"

Matthew, who has been quiet, tells his mother and her friends what just happened. "Well...let's see. Tamara is back and pregnant. Michael just proposed on one knee and has some woman stalking him. Joshua and Alexandra have become officially members of the family, which they might want to think about because there is something always going on, and Michael is still on his way to jail. That's about it."

The four mothers stand there with their mouths wide open. They cannot believe all this has happened in one day. Maxine, James's mother, says, "It looks like you guys' day has been more interesting than ours."

Katherine goes over to hug her new daughter-in-law to be. "Welcome darling to our family. When are you two getting married and... when is the baby due?"

Michael and Tamara both look blank because they have not thought about a wedding date and Tamara has not been to the doctor to find out about her pregnancy. She and Michael do not even know when their baby is coming.

"Mrs. St. John, I do not know when the baby is due because I just took a pregnancy test when I was in Atlanta, and we haven't thought about a wedding date, especially since Michael has to be cleared of this embezzling mess."

Katherine runs her hand through her short hair. "First, there will be no more Mrs. St. John. From now on, I am mom and Alexandra and Joshua we are Aunt Katherine, Doris, Maxine and Cathy to you. Second, Tamara, I will call my OB/GYN Monday so you can just go in for an exam to make sure everything is okay and see how far along you are. Now, as far as the wedding date, you two must decide that."

When she says that, Matt Sr. shrug his shoulders and says casually, "What about Valentine's Day?"

"Mom, that's in three months. We don't have to have a big wedding, but how can we put together something that quick?" Michael frowns and thinks three months is not long enough to plan and have a wedding.

Mike Sr. smiles. "Son, you must have forgotten who you're dealing with. You know these four could put together a royal wedding in three months."

All four women turn to give Mike Sr. a dirty look, and then Katherine goes into diva mode. "Honey, if that's the day you want, that's not a problem with us. Tamara, you need to call your parents to let them know what's going on and next week is Thanksgiving, so see if they can join us here in Memphis. Everyone else here in this room needs to work your schedules where you will be back here by Wednesday or no later than Thursday morning if you can't get a flight back earlier. Michael, we need to use your office. Ladies, we need to plan Thanksgiving dinner for next week and a wedding for February fourteenth."

They go off into Michael's office while everyone else stands there shaking their heads until Alexandra asks with wide eyes, "Are they always like that?"

Matthew laughs. "I told you. You and Joshua might want to think about joining this family. We know our mothers as the divas of shopping and event planning. When there is a party going on, they are all up in the mix. I guarantee you in about...I say one hour they will come back out of the office to tell us dinner will be here, and we will go into Michael's big fancy dining room to have dinner. Anybody want to put up some money that won't happen?"

All the dads say at the same time. "Hell no."

In exactly one-hour, Matthew was right. They have ordered dinner, had it delivered, and when they go into Michael's formal dining room, which seats twenty, they have set the table up so everyone can sit down to eat. They have laid out beverages on his side table with desserts.

All the men are getting the ladies something to drink when Joshua bends over to kiss Alexandra on her forehead to ask her what she wants to drink. "Sweetheart, do you want a glass of wine and if so, do you want white or red?"

"I'll have red Joshua and thank you, sweetie."

Tamara, Christina, and Dianna all look at each other because they wonder what is going on between them. Tamara breaks the silence when she tells everyone she has talked to her parents.

"My mom and dad are so excited about the baby and us getting married, and they say they'll be here Wednesday for Thanksgiving, because they wouldn't miss it for the world. Mom asked Joshua, had I talked to you, and I told her you were here with me in Memphis and that you'll be back for Thanksgiving as well."

"Thanks, sis. I'll make sure Carolyn has my schedule worked out where I'm off Wednesday before Thanksgiving to fly out, and I'll probably go back Sunday night. What about you Alexandra, do you want Carolyn to make the same reservation for you? She has all your information. If that is a time good for you, I'll tell her to book our flights."

Alexandra simply says, "Yes."

Joshua winks at her, and she gives him a smile. Dianna and Tamara cannot wait until they can get her alone to find out what is going on. The conversation around the table went from politics to real estate until Mike Sr. brings up Michael's situation about the embezzlement.

"Okay, guys, we got to put our heads together to figure out who has done this. Everyone at this table knows Michael would not and has no reason to embezzle money from the law firm. We just got to figure out who would want to set him up and why."

"Michael, you know this is no joke you could get disbarred if we don't clear your name. Someone is out to get you, my brother." James gets up to get his wife some more wine. "Who would want to hurt you?"

Tamara sips on her orange juice. "What about Amber? Since she is stalking you, maybe she wants to get rid of you completely, if she can't, have you?"

"Baby, you're so smart. She could want to get rid of me to break us up and this won't be the first time some woman working for us has pulled a stunt like this." Michael bends over to kiss Tamara.

Everyone agrees and thinks back to this time last year when James's assistant, Barbara, had Dianna kidnapped to keep James from being with her. Why wouldn't another woman do something like this again to keep Michael and Tamara from being together?

"What do we do to catch her?" James massages his temples while trying not to think about last year too much.

Michael smiles then get his cell phone out and dials a number. "I know exactly what we need to do. Hey man... what's going on? I need you buddy, and I need you bad."

Chapter Twenty-Nine

Ryan Fields is at home in his L.A. condo when he gets a phone call. He smiles at the number displayed, wondering what is going on now with his law school buddies. "What's up? Man, I swear you guys always have some drama going on. Whose lady has disappeared now?"

Michael laughs out loud. "All of our women are here. This time it is one of us. Someone has set me up for embezzling money from my dad's law firm and I need you to come here to Memphis to help us find out who is doing this to me."

He is one of the sharpest detectives in L.A. and is the one who solved Dianna's kidnapping case last year. Also he was the one who got them into the hospital when Tamara's plane crashed.

"Give me the details." Ryan sits up now because this is serious.

Michael tells him everything that has happened and how they think it might be Amber, but they do not know how to prove it. Michael asks him if he is coming home for Thanksgiving and can he possibly come home early to help him out.

"I was not coming home for Thanksgiving, because I was going to stay here to rest. But since I'm off all this week and next week. I'll catch a flight out tomorrow and we can get on this right away. This ain't no joke, man. I don't want you to be disbarred."

"Thanks, man."

Ryan laughs. "I knew there was some woman involved. You guys know you have women trouble in some way, shape, or form."

"Hey man, that's over. Tamara and I are getting married and she's pregnant, which means we all will be married with kids. So hopefully, the drama is over. See you when you get here."

When he hangs up, Michael tells everyone Ryan will be there tomorrow to help them figure this out. They all are glad because Matthew, James, and Joshua must go back home to get their offices together for them to come back next week for Thanksgiving. They are going to stay a couple of days to help start the investigation and will pick back up when they come back next week.

After dessert, the parents say they are going home and will take their grandkids, who still have not woken up, so the kids can catch up with each other. The ladies clean up the dining room before leaving and the guys fix long island teas, their favorite for after-dinner drinks. Michael put on his other favorite artist *Corinne Bailey Rae* with the lights from the bridge gleaming into the two-story penthouse. The penthouse has nine-foot ceilings with hardwood floors showcasing floor-to-ceiling windows. A view of the Mississippi River sets the scene to be sexy and romantic. Each couple is cuddled up together while a fire is going on in one of the three fireplaces and when *Corinne Bailey Rae's* song 'Breathless' comes on, they dance with each other.

Alexandra automatically looks up at Joshua when his hazel eyes look down at her, because they both are thinking about their lovemaking off that song. He pulls her closer to him an whispers in her ear.

"Baby, I can't stop thinking about us making love. You took me to another level that I have never experienced with anyone else. Sweetheart, do you feel the same?"

"Oh...Joshua, you know I do." Alexandra responds just as Joshua covers her mouth with his when his tongue greets hers and they kiss and kiss. They are so into each other, they forget where they are and who they are with.

Michael cannot help it when he hollers out, "Get a room, Walker."

James raises one eyebrow. "Better still, take your woman in the guest room and handle your business."

Matthew shrugs his broad shoulders because he is out of the loop as usual. "I thought they couldn't stand each other. Oh lord, please do not tell me we have another two people who swear they cannot stand each other and nothing is going on between them. Don't go there. We've been through this already and look at them now. Married with a baby and the other couple pregnant, stalker, and jail."

Everyone laughs because Matthew seldom says things like Michael and James, but he is not joking. He does not want to go through some more drama. The couple is so into each other, Joshua for the first time does not have a comeback. He keeps right on dancing and holding Alexandra close. What everyone does not know is they both are confused about what is going on between them.

Dianna whispers in her husband's ear, "When this song finishes, you need to take your boys up to Michael's office so we girls can talk."

"Mrs. Thomas, are you going to get all up in somebody's business?"

"Hell yeah, and I'm not ashamed to say so. You know I got to find out what is going on with Alexandra and Joshua. Go do your male bonding thing."

James bursts out into laughter when Michael looks over at him and he nods his head toward Michael's office; Michael nods his head in return that he understands. Both men are a little curious to hear from Joshua what is going on as well.

When the song ends, James clears his throat. "Hey guys, let's go to Michael's office so we can talk. We needed to be prepared when Ryan gets here tomorrow. Ladies, I'm sure you want to talk to each other without your men around."

The men head upstairs to Michael's office and before each one goes, they kiss their partners and Joshua kisses Alexandra longer than any of them kiss their women. As they are going up the stairs, Michael laughs at him.

"Can't stand her uh...I know man, the same way I can't stand your sister."

When Alexandra turns around, three pairs of eyes are staring at her with all three women with their hands on their hips. Dianna, of course, breaks the silence.

"Okay girl, you have a lot of explaining to do."

Alexandra half-smiles at her new family. "Where do you want me to start, with the conversations in Atlanta or the one-night stand we had in New York before we came here?"

All three women say at the same time, "One-night stand."

Alexandra and her girls go to sit in front of the fire on Michael's enormous sofa and chairs. Alexandra takes a sip of wine and tells the ladies what has been going on. Even though she's confused about what is happening between them, she really needs to talk to someone to get some feedback on her situation with Joshua.

"First, when we were in Atlanta, you don't know this Tam, but I was calling your brother every night. It started out with me just keeping him posted on you, but we ended up talking for two or three hours every night. We would talk about you, then we would talk about everything from business to art. Then when you came here and I went back to New York. I was so upset about you, the baby, and now Michael is being investigated for embezzlement when I got off the plane. I went straight to Joshua's office. I sat and waited for him for two hours because his assistant would not interrupt his meeting. When he came out and found out I had been sitting there for two hours. He chewed that poor woman out. Then we went to his condo, and I told him what had happened. I started crying and that is when he kisses my tears away. The next thing I know, we are kissing each other, then he sweeps me off my feet to take me into his bedroom and we made love. I have never felt that way with any man before. He made me feel things I did not even know existed. Finally, we got up to take a shower together and I asked him what we were doing, and he told me to let it go and don't think about it. He needed me, and I told him I needed him. We went back to bed after the shower to make love the rest of the night. The next day we caught our flight here and you know the rest."

"Girl, I know about kissing those tears away. That's what got me in trouble and look at me now, engaged and pregnant." Tamara twists her mouth then wrinkles her nose, not believing what has happened between Alexandra and her brother.

"Yeah, but we used condoms. We have not committed to seeing each other seriously, so we will not become engaged to each other." Alexandra gulps down the rest of her wine.

"Alexandra, I know I have not known you long, but I know you're not like these two. You and I are more alike. We like to think and plan things out and really do not live for drama like the two drama queens here. I know this all must be hard for you?" Christina goes over to sit next to her because she can tell she's scared and confused.

Alexandra wraps her arms around herself. "I don't do one-night stands and I do not do drama. Have I been around drama, yes, because I'm friends with Dianna and Tamara, but you're right Chris, that's not me?"

"Well... we can't help it if we like a little excitement in our lives." Dianna high five her buddy Tamara. "But all jokes aside, Alex, how do you feel about Joshua, and what do you want to do?"

Alexandra strokes the back of her neck and then lays her head on the back of the sofa. "I don't know. All I know is he has made me feel like no other man has ever made me feel, but I do not know what I want or if he really wants a relationship. He has been so sweet and concerned about me and it's almost like we are in a relationship, but we are not. Tamara, you know your brother is a straight up player and we have nothing in common. I like the arts, opera, culture, and he likes to drink and party when he is not working twenty-four seven. Joshua does not have a care in the world. When you know I am organized and plan my life out. But there still are some feelings there for him and I don't know if I'm feeling this way because he has been there and protected me with everything going on or I really have some feelings for him."

"Well first, I am sure Carolyn, Joshua's assistant, was in complete shock a woman was at his office for him because he has always kept his private life separate. Second, you and Joshua have a lot in common. He paints, loves the arts, and opera. Joshua is very French, like our mother. He takes to the culture more than I do. Usually, he goes with me or our mother to culture events. Now the straight up player thing you would be correct about that, but you are the first woman I have ever seen my brother display any public affection for. Joshua does not bring any of his playmates around the family. I have run into them with him partying and he acts like they are strangers even then. I know my brother and he have feelings for you. It might confuse him because this would be something he has never dealt with before. Joshua has never been serious about anything but business. Now what you two are going to do about those feelings is going to be interesting to watch."

Dianna smiles. "I say go for it. Just go on and get married and have a baby, then you will be like all of us. You and Joshua make a cute couple and you two would have some pretty babies. I know, we can have a double wedding. Michael and Tamara and you and Joshua. All you must do is go on and get pregnant and we can have a baby shower for the both of you at the same time."

Alexandra and Christina both look at her like she has lost her mind until Alexandra shakes her head. "Dianna, that's crazy as hell. We have never even said we like each other to each other, so why would we be having a baby and getting married."

"Well girl, I think it's established you like each other without you saying it because from those kisses I just witnessed, I would say somebody definitely likes somebody." Dianna laughs out loud because she feels, *here we go again.*

Chapter Thirty

"Before we talk about my life and problems, we're waiting, Joshua, for you to tell us what the hell is going on with you and Alexandra. You know the women are downstairs tearing you apart, so you might as well tell us what's up." Michael twists his lips and sits on the edge of his desk.

Joshua sits on the sofa Michael has slept on many nights after working late, closes his eyes and then opens them to talk to his new best friends and extended family. "Guys, we made love in New York all night before we came here and now, I don't know what's going on with us. I guess we're just kicking it, that's all. She has made me feel like I have never felt with any other woman, but we are not in a relationship. The love making was mind blowing and I feel like I should protect her. I swear I do not know what that is all about. To be honest, I really do not know what the deal is between us, and I guess I'll just have to wait and see what's going to happen next."

"Cool. Now, we need to talk about Michael's situation and what are we going to do?" James leans back with his hands behind his head, accepts what Joshua said and moves on to what is going on right now.

"Michael, I can look over all the financial documents since I deal with money all day. I might see something that stands out which might give us some input on who could do this." Joshua strokes his shadow of a beard.

"That's a good idea Joshua and I'll look at your company documents since I do corporate mergers and James, you can help me with that if you want too." Matthew checks his emails on his iPhone.

"I guess I'll go buy Tamara's engagement ring while you guys are doing your thing." Michael checks his email on his laptop.

"Michael, have you lost your mind?" Joshua's glance sideways raises an eyebrow, not believing he is talking about spending more money. "You can't buy anything. You are under investigation for stealing money, therefore you cannot go out and drop thousands of dollars on a ring. That is why you're in this trouble right now because of your lifestyle. You were the target because you spent money on traveling, shopping, and you were always flying off somewhere. That made it easy for whoever did this to target you."

"Joshua is right. You do not need to do nothing but lie around with your woman until we can figure this out. Do you know what time Ryan will be here?" James asks now and checks his email on his phone.

"Yeah, he just texted me to say he will be on the eleven o'clock flight. He is going to go to his parents first and will call me, so we can meet later. I texted him back to tell him Matt you, and James will pick him up and everybody can meet here. I'm sure the women will have some plans for tomorrow."

The men lock in their plans for tomorrow and talk about besides Amber who would want to set him up and how they can catch them to clear Michael's name. Back downstairs, the women are planning their day for tomorrow. Tamara and Alexandra are going to leave downtown and meet the other women in Cordova where everyone else is staying for Tamara to go to the doctor, shopping, and grocery shopping for Thanksgiving dinner.

Everyone leaves except Joshua and Alexandra because they are staying with Tamara and Michael. They must share the only other extra bedroom because Michael has turned the other bedroom into his home office. They do not mind sharing a room. Alexandra showers first and has on a big tee shirt when Joshua comes to bed with just some pajama bottoms on. She sits in the bed and waits for him with her large gray eyes looking at him.

"Baby, do you feel better now that we are here, and Tamara and Michael are back on track?"

"Yes. I am glad they have worked everything out. Can you believe they are going to get married and have a baby? The two biggest players of all time are settling down."

"I know sweetheart, hopefully all the drama with them will be over and now we all can get back to our everyday life. What are you ladies planning on doing tomorrow?"

Alexandra tells him their plans and they'll be out most of the day. He pulls her into his arms to kiss her with a long goodnight kiss.

"Baby, your kisses make me feel so good."

Alexandra rubs his face. "And your kisses feel good to me, but—"

"You're confused, and you want to just go to sleep and not make love tonight."

Alexandra gasps and stares at him with wide eyes. "How did you know?"

Joshua laughs. "Sweetheart, I know you now and I know you like to know and understand what you're doing and right now. You do not have a clear understanding on what's going on between us."

Alexandra nods her head yes and they both decide on no love-making right now. Joshua agrees with her because he is just as confused and does not understand what is happening between them. They decide they want to wait until they are sure of how they really feel about each other before they cross that line again.

Meanwhile, Michael and Tamara are in the shower where Michael cannot keep his hands off his future wife. Kissing each other until Michael turns her around from him to put her hands on the shower wall enters her from behind.

"Baby, I love you so much. I cannot get enough of you, and I am so glad I can have you every night and every day. You drive me crazy with passion."

Tamara closes her eyes and moans. "Sweetheart, I'm crazy about you and I never want us to be apart again. You are my lover, best friend, and the man I want to spend the rest of my life with."

Michael pulls out of her to turn her around to lift her off her feet, but before he can she slide down his body to grab his hard penis and rubs it while he gets harder and harder and before he can blink an eye. She has put him into her mouth to make love to him. Michael screams out because he was not expecting this and before he completely loses it. He jerks her head up to lift her off her feet to enter her again and lose himself in her. He knows he will never tire of making love to her; she is the only woman who has ever made him feel the way she does. When they finish a long love session in the shower, the couple gets in the bed and Michael tells her the guy's plans for tomorrow and she shares the ladies' plans. Then Tamara wants to know what Joshua said about Alexandra.

"He said they are just hanging out, that's all."

"Michael, you know they are doing more than just hanging out. They have some serious feelings for each other, but don't want to face it." Tamara snuggles up with her lover.

"Baby, I'm not getting into that. They must figure it out just like we did. No one helped us, and we can't help them."

"If you say so."

Michael knows from that comment, the ladies will not stay out of it. They were determined to get Joshua and Alexandra married and with child if it was left up to them.

The next morning, Alexandra and Tamara fix a late breakfast for their guys before going to meet the other ladies. They all sit around enjoying a long lingering breakfast when Tamara asks questions.

"Joshua, did you and Alexandra sleep well?" Tamara's narrow

eyes watch their expression like it is the most common thing for her best friend and brother to be sleeping together.

"Yes, miss nosy. We slept very well." Joshua with a slight close-lipped smile because he knows what his sister is doing.

Alexandra sips on her juice and changes the subject. "What do you two want, a boy or girl?"

Michael, who has been quiet until now, finally says something. "I don't care just as long as it is healthy, and we have our normal life back. I know I'm tired of all the drama we have all been going through these last couple of years."

Joshua pulls Alexandra into his arms and kisses the tip of her nose. "I hear you. From what I have heard. You guys have had some serious drama going on. Alex, baby, do you need any money or my American Express for today?"

"You never ask me anymore if I need money or your Amex card." Tamara raises her eyebrows at her brother's question for Alexandra.

"That's because I quit being responsible for you when you turned eighteen and you have a man to burn up his Amex card."

Alexandra answers his question before sister and brother go back and forth with each other. "No sweetheart, I have my Amex and plenty of money."

When they finish cleaning the kitchen, it is about two o'clock and time for the ladies to leave because all the guys are on their way to Michael's condo. They are going to brainstorm to solve Michael's problem, so he and Tamara can go on with their lives.

All the dads, James, Matthew, and Ryan come in to get down to business and just as they are about to start Tamara and Alexandra, come downstairs to leave. Ryan does not know Alexandra and thinks she is beautiful until he sees Joshua whisper something in her ear then gives her a kiss and a wink when he overhears him saying. "See you when you get home baby, don't spend too much money."

He knows something is going on between them, even though she's not introduced as his woman. Not really knowing Joshua well. He only knows him from the hospital when Tamara's plane crashed, but he has been around these guys long enough to know when they have a relationship going on with one of these women without claiming they are.

He has seen the same thing happen with Michael and Tamara. Joshua is one of their boys, so Joshua is cool with him. The little time he talked to him he is just like Michael and James, not a care in the world, but seems to be a good friend who can be trusted.

"Okay, guys, let us get down to business. Michael, I am going to need everyone's names who work in your office. I've called in a background check on Amber all ready. I know you said she might be the one, but then again, it could always be someone else. An embezzler is usually the most trusted person in the office. We must figure out what reason someone in your office needed more money. That's going to lead us right to the person."

Before anyone can make a comment, Charlie's cell phone rings and he answers with a puzzle look on his face. He talks for about three minutes then hangs up. Everyone looks at him because he smacks his palm against his forehead. James wonders who has called his dad.

"Dad, what's wrong, who was that on the phone?"

"That was your sister, Teresa, who just called to announce she'll be here for Thanksgiving to stay, and she's going to open her medical practice here."

The dads said at the same time, "What!"

"She just calls out the blue, with no warning to say she's moving back to Memphis to open a private practice here and hung up the phone. No reason she suddenly wants to leave Nashville to come back home to live and work." Charlie shakes his head because both his children just do things off the top of their heads.

Teresa Thomas, the same age as Dianna and Christina, is a doctor who lives in Nashville, Tenn. since she graduated from medical school. She also has lived there while doing her residency and then afterwards, she joins a private practice in Nashville and is just as wild as her brother. She is a female version of James. Charlie and Maxine thought they would have no grandchildren if they were depending on their two kids.

"I can't believe your little sister is a doctor. I can remember when she used to run up behind us and now, she can save a human life." Ryan smiles nod thinks about James's sister.

James laughs. "I know. I do not think I would let her crazy butt work on saving my life. Teresa has never had a serious bone in her body. I still can't believe she got that serious about school to become a doctor."

"You don't remember she talked about becoming a doctor? But like you, I ignored her because she was crazy then and probably still crazy now. I guess I'll have to call her Dr. Thomas." Ryan and James laugh because they know even to call Teresa *Dr. Thomas* will not change her personality.

Ryan's cell phone rings and while talking to the person on the other line he pinches his nose, nods his head then takes notes. Ryan is the same height as Michael's six-two with milk chocolate skin, dark amber eyes, a bald head, and a mustache with goatee. His body is slim and tone from working out three to four days a week. He left Memphis to go to Harvard Law School with Michael, James, and Matthew and like James and Matthew, he lives in L.A.

He never crossed his law school buddies' paths until last year when they kidnapped Dianna and he got the case. That was the first time he had seen all of them since law school. He hangs up and looks at everyone. "Guys, you will not believe this."

Chapter Thirty-One

"It seems Ms. Amber Anderson has a restraining order against her with an attorney she worked with in her previous office. She has a problem of falling for the attorneys she works with. My contact talked to the guy and he said she is a nice girl, but she began to stalk him since they worked so close; she took it for something else. He said he thinks that is the reason she wanted to leave Atlanta, because everyone knows." Ryan shakes his head because he does not realize how many crazy women work for men they fall for.

Joshua and James said at the same time, "Man, man, man."

Michael raises one eyebrow. "Ryan, do you think it might be the reason she has tried to set me up? To get back at me because she thought something was going on between us?"

Ryan leans back and looks up, thinking for a minute before speaking. "This could go two ways. She might have done this to get back at every man she felt rejected by, or she just might be a person who does nothing but work and get work relationships confused with personal relationships and really think you two are in a relationship. I need to dig a bit more into her background, but I still want a list of everyone who works for you. Michael, right off the top of your head, who do you trust the most in your office?"

Michael answers without hesitation. "Bruce Newman. I've known him since Harvard law, as an undergrad, and he's a partner and the office manager of the law firm."

"When you say *office manager*, what do you mean?" Ryan frowns and need to get a clear understanding. "Does he just manager the office and not practice at all?"

"Well, besides being a partner and practicing attorney, he's over the office, which includes hiring and firing, payroll, billing hours, and anything pertaining to running the business side and not just the law side."

"Mmm." Ryan writes Bruce's name and functions. "I'm going to do some background checks on him just to be safe."

Joshua's cell phone rings and when he answers, he frowns and rubs his temple because the person on the other end is saying something not making him happy. When he finishes his conversation, he looks at everyone. "Guys, that was Carolyn, my assistant, and I have three hours to get to the airport to catch a flight back to New York because one of my major clients has a financial crisis and as his investment banker, I got to go because it could ruin his life, which will lead to ruining mine. I'll be back next week."

Joshua rushes upstairs to pack and James said he would drop him off at the airport. The guys and the dads sit around discussing a game plan to get everything in place to clear Michael's name. They have just come downstairs when all the ladies pull up and insist; they help them unload their cars.

Katherine and Doris give out orders while they hold their two grandkids. They both speak to Ryan and tell him to grab a bag and to come over Thanksgiving for dessert. Michael stares at all the food and wonders what is going on.

"Mother... why do you have all this food and why are you bringing it into my house?"

"Because darling, we're having Thanksgiving dinner here, that's why."

"What! Tamara, why are we hosting Thanksgiving dinner this year?"

Before Tamara can answer, Doris is standing there with her hands on her hips, still giving out orders. "Michael, your dining room table holds twenty and there is room to set up other tables if we need to. That's what you get for having this huge penthouse."

Tamara realizes she does not see her brother, but she must tell Michael her news first. "Baby, I saw the doctor and everything is fine, and she said our due date is June 15th . By the way, where is Joshua?"

"You're doing okay, and everything is fine with you and our baby?"

"Yes honey, we both are fine, but where is Joshua?"

"He had a business emergency and had to leave for New York right away. He said he would see us next week."

Tamara turns to look at Alexandra and can tell she is disappointed, and the other ladies notice also, so they take her into the kitchen to talk.

"Are you alright Alex?" Dianna asks, because she can see she looks strange.

"I'm fine. We are not a couple, so he does not have to tell me his every move. This is what I mean, Joshua and I would not work, because he is used to being free and jumping from city to city telling no one and I can understand because I do not tell anyone my schedule. I'm a flight attendant and he's an international entrepreneur. It would not work between us." Alexandra walks out of the kitchen before any of the ladies can say a word. When she is out of sight, they discuss their friend's situation.

"Was that how Michael and I were when we were saying we were just friends?"

"Hell yes." Dianna munch on a candy bar. "You two could not see what everyone else saw. That's the same thing happening with those two. Alex and Josh have feelings for each other, but don't want to face it."

Christina eats her candy bar and also jumps into the conversation. "And just like you two, they're going to have to figure it out themselves. I just wonder what type of drama is going to go on for them to find out they care about each other."

"You know Alex has a point about both being free. Alexandra has been on her own since she was twenty with no immediate family, and Joshua has been playing around and carefree all his life. Alex had to take things seriously, whereas Josh has taken nothing serious in his life except business. It might be hard for them to be together."

All the women are quiet because maybe it's not meant for them to be together. Before they can say anything else Kennedy and Zachary run into the kitchen straight to their moms for some attention. With their dads, Matthew and James following them.

James glances at all the women and knows something is up just as Michael walks in looking for Tamara. "What's going on? Why are you looking that way and where is Alexandra?"

"Darling, do not worry about us, we're fine." Dianna grabs her husband by the waist.

"Christina, are you ladies in here all in Joshua and Alexandra business?" Matthew asks his wife.

"No." Christina does not say another word.

"Tamara...stay out of it." Michael turns to his fiancée.

"Of course, baby. We'll stay completely out of it." Tamara reaches up to give him a kiss.

All three men stand there as their women stare directly at them without blinking an eye and agree with them to not get in Alexandra and Joshua's business. They all have the same smile on their faces and act like they are not concerned one bit about their other friend's love life.

James shrugs his broad shoulders. "Come on guys. We might as well leave because they will not tell us the truth. We all know our women, and that was too easy for them to agree not to be in Alexandra and Joshua's business."

All the guys go out of Michael's kitchen and shake their heads as their women go back to their conversation on what is going on with their friend and Tamara's brother.

Dianna cannot wait until they leave. "I'm telling you those two need a little push."

Tamara agrees with her friend. "Both are so hardheaded they really think they dislike each other."

Christina waits a minute before she says, "Just like you and my brother swore you were just friends for two years, we can't push them together. Like we couldn't push you two together."

They all agree they cannot push them together, so they are going to wait and see what happens when everyone is together for Thanksgiving because something will go on with this family because it is never a dull moment.

Chapter Thirty-Two

The next day, Ryan works from his dad's home office when he gets the call he was waiting for. His friend, Steve Johnson, who is a detective with Memphis Police Department, grew up with him and they hang out together when he's in L.A.

"Steve, what's up, man?"

"Man, I didn't know you knew the St. Johns this well to be volunteering to work on this case."

"Yeah, Michael and I went to law school together and used to hang out tough in our partying days. I want to help clear him because Michael has no reason to steal money, especially from his own law firm."

"Well, things look like he did. Do you think someone is purposely setting him up?" Steve reads over the file assigned to him.

"Hell yeah. Michael St. John was a straight up player that all the women love, and he loves to party, travel, and shop, but he is not a criminal. His parents are rich, why would he steal from his own folks when they have and would give him anything he wants? Michael might seem like he is stealing money because I can guarantee you. I have not seen the file, but I know my friend and I bet his expenses are crazy. But that's Michael, he would jump on a plane in a minute. That's why whoever is framing him is using his lifestyle to set him up."

"That could be true, but I'm also looking at a record of his Black Card American Express statement and it's something serious. He just had about twenty-five thousand dollars charged to his card about six weeks ago in one day, but they were all women shops, so his girl must have had a shopping spree." Steve's mouth is wide open while he looks at his credit card statement because he does not love any woman that much.

Ryan laughs. "That's Tamara, who he is going to marry and she probably went shopping because she lost everything in a plane crash. She survived last month. Bottom line, all of them and their women have money that none of them must steal. Whoever did this knows about Michael's lifestyle, which is why they set him up to be the fall guy. Think about it, if Michael were low key and just worked all the time, it would not make sense for him to need to steal any money, for what? They picked him because he's always on a jet, at a party, or at some store shopping."

"You know you're right, but who do you think in his office would do this?"

"That's what you and I are going to find out. They think it might be Amber Anderson who just started at the firm and has been stalking Michael. Plus, I had a contact in Atlanta, where she is from to check her out. She has a restraining order against her for stalking one attorney there."

"I can hear in your voice you don't think it's her."

Ryan looks out his dad's home office window. "You would be correct. First, she really does not know Michael's lifestyle that well. She just started with the firm so how would she know how much he flies all around the world, parties, or even his shopping habits? But what disturbs me the most is how did an attorney with a restraining order even get hired to work there?"

Steve sits up because his friend is on to something. "You know, you're right. Who would hire someone with that against them to work in a law firm unless they had a reason? Who does the hiring there?"

Ryan grins. "That's it, man. Michael said Bruce Newman, who is a partner and office manager, does the hiring. I need you to find out if Bruce hired her. If he did, then we need to check him out good because why would a partner even hire someone who has a restraining order against them unless he really didn't know it existed?"

Both men know they are on to something. Steve said he will get right on it and when he gets the information, they will get together to plan their next step. Ryan said he is going to do some research on his own and they agree to meet for dinner at six.

Steve sits at the bar at TGI Friday's restaurant in Cordova by the Wolf Chase Mall, where he agreed to meet Ryan. It is after six and Ryan has not made it yet but has texted him to tell him he is on his way. He sips on his drink and watches the sports channel; he does not see Ryan come in until he hears his voice.

"Sorry man, I got caught up on the phone and the time slipped up on me. You want to grab a seat so we can eat and talk?"

The two men put in their food orders and discuss what both have found out about this case.

Steve is still sipping on his drink. "You were right, Bruce Newman hired Amber, and it seems Michael had nothing to do with it. He left everything up to him."

"That's interesting. I checked out Bruce and so far, he is clean and seems really dedicated to the law firm. I am still not sure if Amber is the one; she is financially secure so if she did it, it would be for revenge against Michael because he does not want her. Which would be a good reason for someone with a twisted mind, but I still want to check out everyone who works in the office."

"I know women who have done some crazy things. It could be her or someone else who knows about Amber and want everyone to think that it's her."

Ryan smiles. "That is exactly what I am thinking. It might not be Amber, it could be some other woman who wants Michael that he has paid no attention to. They all have a track record of crazy women working for them, so this will not be the first time. Let us check everybody out, especially all the female employees."

Ryan and Steve eat their dinner and decide they must get on top of things quickly, so Ryan can return to L.A. when his vacation is over and not have to stay any extra days to help solve this case.

Meanwhile, everyone has gone back home so they can be back in Memphis this Wednesday or no later than Thursday morning for Thanksgiving. Michael and Tamara have just been relaxing because she has morning sickness again. They have been lying around watching movies and reading.

Michael hates to see her so sick. "Baby... are you sure we shouldn't call the doctor?"

"No, it's just morning sickness; every pregnant woman goes through it. I just don't feel like doing anything."

Michael decides right then he will have the cleaning service he uses to come in Tuesday to clean his condo because he does not want Tamara to lift a finger. All the moms are at his house Wednesday morning before Thanksgiving to cook. Tamara wants to help, but the moms and Michael insist she does not need to do anything. All the food is there at Michael's house for them to cook there so they do not have to transport food from their homes to Michael's condo. That way Thursday they can just show up, heat all the food, and enjoy their day with family and friends.

Wednesday afternoon everyone arrives back in Memphis. Tamara's parents are staying with the St. John's in Cordova along with Matthew, Christina, and Zachary. James, Dianna, and Kennedy are staying with Dianna's mother since Teresa James's sister is back and has moved back in with their parents until she can find a condo to live in. Joshua and Alexandra are going to stay with Michael and Tamara, and they were to arrive downtown at two that afternoon.

Michael's doorbell rings, and Tamara runs to the door to see her brother and her other best friend, but when she opens the door, she steps back. "Alex, where is Joshua?"

"Hey girl." Alexandra hugs her friend and waves at Michael.

"Who knows? All I know is when I got to JFK he was nowhere to be seen, and his seat next to me on the plane was empty. You know your brother; there is no telling where he is or what he's doing."

"Baby, have you talked to my brother and is he still coming?" Tamara hollers out to Michael, who is laying on the couch watching a football game and never looks up.

"No."

"No, you have not talked to him or no he's not coming?"

Michael looks up and frowns. "No, I have not talked to him, and I don't know if he's still coming because I have not talked to him."

"I can't believe him." Tamara gets her cell phone out of her pocket of her jeans to call her brother. "His voice mail is coming right on. If Joshua does not show up for our first family Thanksgiving dinner together as a family. I am going to kill him. He knows he has missed holiday dinners in the past, but this is different because we are blending families together for the first time and he needs to be here for that. If he's working on some business deal and just forgot. I'm going to kill your man."

"Hey...that's your brother and you know how he is, especially with business. He might show up and he might not." Alexandra takes off her leather coat to hang it up on the coat rack.

"He better show up and he better be on time because if he doesn't, I'm going to tell mommy and she'll cuss him out in English and French and he definitely don't want to get on our mother's unpleasant side."

"Joshua has always put work before anything else...that's another reason we couldn't be together. You never know when he will show up or not show."

"I know, but this is different, and I bet if you two were together he would put you before work."

Alexandra just looks at her friend and shakes her head because she is not going to even make a comment to that since nothing she can say will change her mind.

Chapter Thirty-Three

Thanksgiving afternoon everyone is at Michael and Tamara's condo except Joshua. The women have cooked a traditional southern Thanksgiving dinner for everyone to enjoy. Just as Mike Sr. blesses the table, the doorbell rings and Michael gets up to answer it. He opens the door and there stands his buddy and future brother-in-law.

"Man, you're in big trouble. Your woman pissed; your sister, your mother, and the rest of the women probably want to strangle you. I would hate to be in your shoes right now." Michael laughs at him.

Joshua rubs his eyes and moves slowly because he has not slept in two days. "Man, I have been through hell with that client. I just barely caught this flight out. Are they real mad?"

"Hell yeah. I suggest you dig deep for all your charm to get out of this one."

The two fine men walk back into the dining room where everyone is waiting to see who is at the door. When he walks in, everyone pauses and looks. Joshua walks in to kiss his mother on both cheeks and then goes right over to Alexandra to ask for her forgiveness.

He bends down in front of her. "Baby, I'm so sorry. I missed the flight because I was still tied up with the client I had to leave out for earlier when we were here. I just left him and went straight to the airport. Please forgive me."

Teresa leans over whispers to her sister-in-law Dianna. "Who the hell is that? He's fine as hell."

"Taken... even though they don't know it yet, but they're a couple."

"I can tell big time. Brother came straight in begging for forgiveness from her."

Alexandra glances up at him and she can see the bags under his eyes; for the first time, he looks exhausted. "Yes, I forgive you sweetheart. Have a seat so we can eat."

James waggles his eyebrows crack on him. "Hey man, what about the rest of us? Don't you want us to forgive you too?"

Everyone laughs because only James would say something like that, and Michael must jump in on the conversation. "It's obvious we don't matter. Brother came right in and straightened things out with I guess who's the most important one at this table."

Joshua relaxes because he is back to his self. "And you know it. I know how to get out of the doghouse. You guys are important, but I got enough sense to know who's really the most important one here, and it's not you two."

James cocks his head to the side. "That's cold, man. I thought we were your boys. I can't believe we don't rank up there with your woman."

Mike Sr. taps his wine glass. "Well, now that's settled, as I was going to say before being interrupted. We are so blessed this year to have everyone here and to have new family members: Adrienne, Thomas, Joshua, Tamara, and Alexandra. Welcome to the family and we're glad to have Teresa back home to stay. We also are happy to be sharing our first Thanksgiving with our grandchildren Zachary Nigel and Kennedy Dianna and the new one that's on its way."

Everyone toasts their glasses, and dinner has officially begun. Matt Sr. starts the conversation off. "I hope to go into this New Year we will not have any more drama. Please ladies, do not disappear on any of your men again. I swear if one more woman disappears in this family Mike, Charlie and now you Thomas, along with myself will tie all you women up with your man because we're not looking for or waiting for one more person to show up."

All the guys said. "Amen."

The women look at them like they are crazy because they do not understand what the problem is. Dianna, who is the queen of disappearing, simply states, "We do not disappear. We just needed to get away. Cannot help it when we get away you guys do not know where we are. I call it being in solitude when you guys think of it as disappearing. Anyway, Teresa, are you really moving back to Memphis?"

Teresa has been gone from Memphis for the last eight years after graduating college and medical school in Nashville, TN. She is an OB/GYN who is petite like her mother at five-five, pecan skin color, curly black hair that passes her shoulders and the same light brown bedroom eyes she shares with her brother, James. That is not all she shares with him. She is just like he was in the past, a true player. She never had a serious boyfriend in her life. From just liking to play around with different guys, she feels it keeps down the conflict in her life. She also was serious about her schooling to become a doctor, so she really did not have the energy or time to commit to a relationship. That is why she is carefree with relationships and settling down.

"Girl, yes. I'm going to set up my practice, buy me a condo and for me that is as settled as I plan to be. No marriage or babies for me, I will just be Auntie Teresa. I will baby-sit when I am not partying or traveling. I guess I'm going to have to find me some new party buddies here in Memphis and LA since the two biggest players of all time have settled down." Teresa laughs and points her finger at James and Michael, who she still cannot believe they both have stopped messing around.

"Some people grow up, Teresa. I guess you're just never going to become a responsible person." Charlie presses his lips together at his youngest child.

"Daddy, I am responsible. Didn't you hear me just say I'm going to buy a condo and start my business? How much more responsible can you get?"

Maxine answers for her husband. "Honey, he meant having a family. I'm not complaining because for a while there I thought we would have no grandchildren, so one child married is better than nothing."

Everyone laughs while the ladies clear the table, so they can have dessert and after-dinner drinks. The men fix the drinks while the ladies serve desserts. Just as everyone has their drinks and dessert, the doorbell rings again, and it is Ryan who they have invited over for dessert.

"What's up man you're just in time for drinks, dessert, and football?" Michael gives him their man embrace.

"Hey guys, my timing was perfect." Ryan looks over and spots Teresa. "Dr. Thomas, what's up?"

Teresa smiles. "Ryan Fields, what are you doing here? I thought you lived in L.A.?"

"I had to come home to save Michael's butt from being kicked out of the judicial system. You know your family always has some type of drama going on with their lives." Ryan goes over to give her a hug.

Teresa and Ryan stand there hugging each other until Teresa steps back to look at him. "You look good. So...is there a Mrs. Ryan Fields?"

James and Michael burst out laughing because they know Teresa is being her usual self of flirting.

"No. Is there a Mr. Thomas in your life?"

"Of course not, darling. I don't have time for a husband. Come... join me in the great room so we can catch up with each other." Teresa takes Ryan by the arm and escorts him out of the room.

"Honey, suppose we women want you guys to stay in here and talk with us?" Tamara grabs Michael around the waist to stay. "You can watch football anytime. You guys need to spend this time with your women."

"Tamara, don't you know that's what men do on Thanksgiving. We eat, drink, and watch football... all weekend." Joshua bends over to give Alexandra a kiss then follows all the other men.

"Let them go...cause that's why all their credit cards are going to be burning rubber tomorrow because it's the biggest shopping day of the year. This is our favorite time of the year, so if you guys want to watch football all weekend. You need to drop those credit cards right on that table." Katherine stands there with her hands on her hips.

"Oh hell... let's get out of here before they talk us into mortgaging our homes for them to shop all day and night." Thomas knows how much money his wife spends the day after Thanksgiving, so he is afraid if all the women are together spending their money. They will go broke.

"Dad, don't be that way. Give your wife that black card." Joshua laughs at his father.

"Joshua, you need to be quiet because you don't have a wife. You don't even have a serious girlfriend so you're not spending a dime." His father crosses his arms, not believing his son is messing with him.

"Hey...Alexandra is my baby. Alex... do you want my Black Amex?"

Dianna speaks up before Alexandra can say anything. "If she doesn't want it, I'll take it because we can use all the plastic we can get for tomorrow." Dianna and Alexandra bump fists.

Matthew and James both push Joshua out the room when Matthew says, "Man, you need to leave that alone because I'm telling you, you do not know those women. Especially all our mothers. They're serial shoppers on a regular day so you know they cut up on the biggest shopping day of the year."

Chapter Thirty-Four

As the men get comfortable in front of Michael's huge flat screen TV while all their women plan their shopping day and what stores they are going to hit first. Even though Christina, Dianna, Alexandra, Tamara, and Teresa do not shop like the moms, they are looking forward to a day of shopping and leaving the kids with the guys. Finally, about nine, everyone leaves except Joshua and Alexandra, who are staying with Michael and Tamara.

Tamara and Alexandra go straight to bed because they are getting up at five in the morning to meet everyone at Katherine's house. Michael and Joshua are watching the sports channel and drinking brandy.

"Hey man, have you and Alex taken your relationship to the next level yet?" Michael lies on one couch while Joshua is on the other one.

"I have not talked to her until today, because I'm serious Michael. I have been locked up in a conference room since I left here dealing with my client. You know me and Alex, we just deal with each other when we see each other. We're cool."

"Hmm." Michael sips on his drink. "Yeah, I remember that we're just cool stage."

They watch one more game and call it a night because all the guys are coming back to Michael's tomorrow to watch football and eat because that is where all the food leftovers are. They figure if they want to eat, they need to be where the food is.

Joshua goes into the bedroom he shares with Alexandra to take off his jeans, cashmere sweater, and Gucci loafers to grab a pair of pajamas bottom out of his luggage so he can get in the bed. Alexandra knocked out, and he automatically pulls her into his arms. She moans, and he kisses her forehead and passes out himself.

Michael woke up about ten the next morning in a panic because Tamara is not in the bed with him. He jumps up, slips on his sweats and tee shirt, then runs downstairs where Joshua sits at the table with some sweats and tee shirt on also reading the morning paper.

"Where is she?"

"Who?"

"Tamara. Where is she, Joshua?"

Joshua laughs. "Chill out, man. Alex gone too, so I'm going to assume they gone shopping. They must have got up incredibly early while we were still asleep."

Michael let out a deep breath. "I'm sorry, man, but I just had a flashback of when she disappeared for all those weeks. You don't know what it's like to have the woman you love just to be gone. You wake up and she's gone, and you can't talk to her or see her because you don't know where she is."

Joshua is quiet because he does not understand since he has never been in love and has had no one to disappear on him. Before he can say anything, Michael's cell phone rings and Michael smiles before he answers.

"Good morning, baby. Yes, I just got up," he laughs. "Yes baby, I was wondering where you were. Okay...have fun shopping. I love you too."

"Wow. She knew what you were feeling, that's deep." Joshua sits there, unable to move because his sister called him and knew what he was going through.

199

"And that, my friend, is genuine love. When you can feel each other even when you're not with each other."

Before Michael can say anything else, the doorbell rings. In walks James with Kennedy and Matthew with Zachary, along with the dads and Ryan. They will spend the day watching football, drinking, and eating. About five in evening, Tamara, Dianna, Christina, Teresa, and Alexandra come in with Chinese takeout because they know their men will want something else to eat because they have been eating on leftovers all day.

Tamara runs straight to Michael and jumps in his lap, kisses him all over his face. "Baby, I missed you today. I'm tired, rub my feet."

Dianna walks over to kiss her husband and pick up their daughter, who looks like she has eaten and drunk too much. "Isn't that cute? They are still new and cannot stand to be away from each other. James, what have you been feeding our daughter all day?"

Christina bends over to kiss Matthew and to get Zachary, who yawns. "Girl, I know that's right our poor babies look like they are about to burst. Matthew, I know you did not give him something every time he asked for it?"

James and Matthew both shrug their broad shoulders when Matthew's reply. "Baby, we just wanted to make them happy, so we might have given them maybe too much, but we didn't know."

"James, you did not give these kids everything you guys have been eating?" Dianna looks at all the men, including the dads who look like they have done nothing wrong.

"Baby, we didn't give them any cokes, only water." James crosses his arm across his chest.

Alexandra stands in the corner and looks when Joshua gets up and comes over to give her a kiss. "How was your day baby, did you enjoy yourself?" He runs his finger down her petite nose and then gives her a long kiss.

She does not know why, but she feels better after he kisses her and asks about her day. "Yes, it was a lot of fun, but I'm tired. We left them still shopping."

The dads have been quiet until she said that Mike Sr. head quickly comes up and squints his eyes. "You left them still shopping. Guys, we won't have a dime when they finish spending our money."

Charlie comes out the kitchen narrow eyes, looks around and realizes he does not see their wives. "Oh hell, they still out shopping. Why didn't you guys drag them back here with you?"

Everyone laughs while the men start back watching the game and the women go into the kitchen to talk. The guys follow them to fix their plates and take the food back in the great room to eat while the women sit in the kitchen talking and eating.

"Alex, why don't you and Josh just tell everyone that you are boyfriend and girlfriend? You guys are sleeping together, and act seriously involved with each other. You might as well make the announcement because we already know what's going on." Tamara slightly tucks chin chews on her egg roll.

"For your information, Joshua and I have not had sex with each other since that one night and we can't tell you we're boyfriend and girlfriend, because we're not. We talked and have decided not to have sex again until I understand what is going on with us. The funny thing about that is he surprised me when he told me he knew that was the reason for us not to have sex. He said he knew me and knew I did not want to cross the line again until I knew what was going on with us. I didn't think he understood me at all, and I found out not only does he understand me but has accepted it."

Dianna stops midway with her fork. "You mean to tell us you're sleeping in the same bed together and have not touched each other. Now, I'm really confused with you two."

"Probably after Thanksgiving. I will not see your brother again until your wedding Tamara and I'm tired of trying to figure him out. He knows we cannot go any further because that is just not me to have one-night stands. I do not sleep around unless I am in a relationship with the person, or at least trying to work on developing a relationship with them. Joshua has not shown he wants a relationship, and I will not be someone he can just hookup with when he feels like it or makes the time to just get laid. I have never been one to do something like that not knowing what is going on with the situation. He'll go his way and I'll go mine." Alexandra picks up her glass to drink her juice.

All the women are quiet because she has a point. They leave it alone. Joshua and Alexandra both are stubborn and only they can make this work if that is something they want to happen.

Chapter Thirty-Five

The rest of the weekend, all the guys bond over sports and the women shop and plan Tamara and Michael's February wedding. Everyone heads to the airport Sunday afternoon to go back home except Ryan. He stays a few more days to solve the case of who is setting Michael up for embezzlement. Monday morning Ryan meets Michael and all the dads at Mike Sr. house, so he can go over what he has done so far. He lets them know he and Steve are working extremely hard to find out who did this.

"I know you think Amber did this, but just like Dianna's case, whoever did this, they had to know Michael about your life to frame you. Just like the kidnapper had to know who Dianna was, what time she was going to be at the airport and what James's Jeep looked like to kidnap her, it is the same thing. To frame you with embezzlement someone must know you jet hop, party, and shop, because that would be the reason you need more money to support your lifestyle. Amber just met you so she would not know that in full details." Ryan yawns because he had gone out partying with Steve last night.

Charlie is impressed this young man is so sharp. "So, it might not be Amber, but it must be someone in the office who knows Michael's lifestyle well. Which could be anyone?"

Michael agrees. "Everyone who works there knows I'm in and out from traveling, partying, and everyone knows I like to look good. They also know I stay downtown in an expensive condo and drive a Jaguar. So how are we going to find out which one is framing me?"

"Michael, I need you to think. Who might need some money in your office. Have you heard anyone talking about money or need to make some more money?" Ryan wants him to think about this.

Michael sits there for a minute to think and then closes his eyes and takes a deep breath because what he just realizes, he does not want to believe. "Ryan, I just thought about something, and I guess I just didn't want to face this. But...Lisa, my assistant just came to me recently asking for a raise because she is a single mother with two boys and her ex-husband has stopped paying child support and she told me point blank she needs some more money. I guess I blink it out because I didn't want to think she could do this to me."

Charlie shakes his head. "Oh hell, not another woman who works for one of you guys pulling another stunt. We should have learned from James last year about your personal assistant."

"Michael, does Lisa handle all your personal affairs, like to keep up with your business and personal expenses?" Ryan pinches his nose, thinking *here we go again* with some woman losing it over one of them.

"That's just it. Lisa knows about my finances and lifestyle better than me. She knows how I spend money and all my credit card charges because she is the one who stays on top of me to pay my personal bills. Hell... I just had her to pay some bills for me because of what I was going through with Tamara. I keep a checkbook in my desk to pay bills when she tells me because I'll forget, so I had her to go into my office and pay bills for me recently."

Ryan rubs a hand across his bald head. "Here's the thing. It must be someone who knows you and your lifestyle to pin this on you. Michael, I must ask you this question because this is almost the same thing happened to James. Does this woman like you?"

"Honestly Ryan, I don't know. She has never crossed the line or acted like she had any personal interest in me, but neither did Barbara. But look what she did. Man, I can't believe Lisa would do this."

"Well, James couldn't believe Barbara would have done what she did, but now she's in jail for kidnapping charges all because she was in love with him." Matt Sr. twists his lips.

"Like I told you guys when it happened to James, it must be someone who knows everything. Michael, if Lisa is in love with you and needs money bad, she might set you up for two reasons. First, she knows Tamara is special to you. She is not like all the rest of the women you have played around with in all the years she has worked for you. She might set you up for revenge, and then it also seems like she really needs the money."

Michael stares down at his Bally shoes. "What do we do now? If it is not Amber and you think it's Lisa, how do we catch her?"

Ryan smiles for the first time. "That's easy. We are going to do a serious background check on her. We will find out where she shops, where she banks, what school her kids attend and how much it costs. When we finish, we will know everything about Lisa. This will tell us why she needs some money more than anyone else. Remember, embezzling is stealing money, so someone needs more money than they are making for whatever reason. Steve and I think we know who it is, but we might be wrong with finding out this recent information. I will say nothing else until we finish with our investigation, and I think we will have your embezzler. I must wrap this up, so I can get back to L.A. and get me some rest until the next set of drama comes up with you guys."

Matt Sr. shakes his head no. "We have already told them no more drama. Michael is going to get married, and they will have their baby next year in June and no more disappearing women, plane crashes, business falling apart or kidnapping. We're going into the next year drama free."

Ryan grabs his chocolate brown Ralph Lauren trench coat and laughs. "You wish. You know, with these guys, them, and their women live for drama. I need to go meet Steve because we must go back to the drawing board. Lisa really might be the one who is doing this, so we have got to regroup to wrap this up. I'll call you, Michael, as soon as I know something."

Chapter Thirty-Six

Michael goes home to find Tamara sitting there looking out the window. She is staring into space. He immediately goes over to her because he is afraid she is going into a depression about everything that has been happening.

"Baby, what's wrong?"

She looks up because she did not realize he was there. "Baby, what's going to happen if Ryan can't clear you? I'm scared, Michael, you might have to go to jail."

Michael gathers her into his arms. "Sweetheart, you do not have to worry about that. Ryan is going to find out who is doing this, and everything will get back to normal and we can go on with our lives. Baby, I have something to tell you concerning the embezzling case."

"What is it?"

"I just finished talking with Ryan and he made me think about something. I had totally blinked this out because I guess I didn't want to face it."

Michael goes into full details of what he just told Ryan and how Ryan thinks it could be Lisa because she might have feelings for him, and she needs more money.

Tamara hands over her mouth. "Michael, please tell me there is not another woman trying to destroy someone's life because of their feelings. What is it you guys keep hiring a bunch of crazy women? Dianna was kidnapped last year because of James' crazy assistant, and you have hired a stalker with Amber who might have done this or your assistant who knows all your business."

"Baby, we can't help it the women love us." Michael laughs to change the mood.

Tamara gives him a fake smile, crosses her arms. "That's not funny. Michael, these women have tried to destroy our lives. If Ryan does not solve this, you could go to jail or be disbarred, and you know you love to practice law. Plus, I am not taking care of no man, not even you."

"Baby, you wouldn't take care of me? I'll take care of you. Speaking of that, have you decided if you're going to start flying again?"

It seems like their entire lives are up in limbo. And that's why Tamara was staring out of the window. "Right now, I'm too sick with morning sickness to fly. I think... I'm going to take a leave of absence until after I have the baby, and then I might go back part time like Dianna. Baby... are we going to live here or New York?"

Michael closes his eyes because they have a lot to figure out. "I know we must stay here until we get everything straight concerning the embezzlement. I want to still run the law firm, but wherever my family is that's where I'll live so it's up to you."

Tamara cuddles up to him, thinks for a minute. "I think we should live here so you can keep running the law firm. We can keep my condo in New York so when we go there and visit my folks, we will have somewhere to stay instead of hotels or at my parent's house. When I start flying again, I can always fly out of anywhere to do my flights. I feel so much better now we that have settled some of our life."

Thank you, baby. I will move anywhere... as long as we're together, but I'm glad you want to live here. Do not forget we have the house in Key West also to get away and I was thinking about buying a condo in L.A., so we will have somewhere for our family to stay when we are out there. Does that sound good?"

"Yes. That sounds great because I fly in and out of L.A. a lot and that way our family will have our own space. We might have to move out of this condo when the baby comes because we will not have a guest room for family because we will need the guest bedroom for a nursery. Honey, I'm hungry let us go fix something to eat." Tamara pulls Michael up, so they can go into the kitchen to fix dinner.

"After dinner, can you give me my dessert?" Michael stops her, grabs her in his arms before they go into the kitchen. "I need some loving baby. You have been feeling so bad, a brother been on lockdown and I am missing it something awful. Make love to me, baby."

Michael kisses Tamara up and down her neck as he pulls her shorts and panties down at the same time. Feeling her, he feels her wet and ready for him, which makes him become hard instantly. He kisses her long and hard and both moan when Tamara unzips his pants and right there between the living room and kitchen Michael picks her up while presses her back up against the wall and enters her in one swift move.

"Baby, I need this, I miss you. I can't go this long without having you." Michael's eyes close, head leaned to the back while Tamara wraps her long legs around his waist and holds on to his broad shoulders for life.

"Michael...Michael, it feels so good. I love you, baby, I love you."

"Baby, there is not a word that's been invented to tell you how I feel about you. Tamara, I love you so much, you are my world and if you ever leave me, my world would end."

They make love up against the wall until both climax and then Michael picks her up to take her upstairs to their bedroom where he loves his woman the rest of the night.

The next day, Ryan calls to ask Michael a couple more questions about Lisa and to tell him they are down to the end. He and

Steve have a couple more things to check out and they think they will have solved it.

"Ryan, do you think it really was Lisa?"

"I don't know right now but with what we are gathering, it could possibly be her. Hang in there, buddy, we are about to wrap this up so you can go on with your life. Man, your playing days are over now that you're getting ready to be a husband and daddy."

"I love that woman so much I can't wait. It's over, no more playing around for me. There is no other woman on this earth who makes me feel the way Tamara does and to get the bonus of having a baby with her. I couldn't ask for nothing else in this life."

"Wow. That must be love."

Michael smiles into the phone. "That, my brother... it is."

Chapter Thirty-Seven

The next day, Ryan and Steve sit outside on Michael's office parking lot waiting for someone to come out. Both have an idea now who it is from all the information they have collected, and now they must see if their hunch is right. If they follow them to where they think they are going to go. They will have solved the case. Embezzlers usually have a serious reason for doing what they do, and what they dug up will be the primary reason someone would steal money and set someone else up to take the fall.

"Bingo." Ryan looks up just in time from his iPhone.

"Damn man...you're good. If you ever want to come back home, you have a place on the force as my partner because you know your stuff." Steve pulls out slowly so they can follow them without being noticed. "Or if you ever want to open a PI firm, let me know because I would love to be your partner."

Ryan laughs. "Man, working for Michael and James with all the crazy stuff they have going on. I swear it has made me want to open a private practice just for their drama. They know they have some stuff going on that somebody always needs something investigated."

"You got to be kidding me? Do they really have that much going on you could set-up a private practice?"

"Hell yeah. I could have made an arm and a leg off them in the last two years."

Both men laugh as they slowly follow the car and know they are about to wrap this up. Ryan can catch his flight out tomorrow back to L.A. where he will wait for his college and law school buddies to call him for their next adventure. They follow the car to a part of town where either man would usually not go to. Both have been in law enforcement long enough to know what happens when someone goes there.

"I can't believe someone would ruin their entire life because of this." Steve parks his car out of sight.

"I know. Some people just make the wrong choices in life which end up destroying their entire lives."

Both men sit and wait until they see what they are waiting for, and both say at the same time. "Gotcha."

Seven o'clock that night Michael gets a call from Ryan for him and the dads to meet him at 201 Poplar at the Criminal Justice Center downtown. He wants them to come to the top floor where the detectives are because they have the embezzler. Michael immediately calls his dad, and he tells him they will stop by his house to pick him up since he already lives downtown.

"Tamara." Michael hollers out to her when he gets off the phone.

She walks back in the great room wide-eyed and wonders why he is shouting for her. "What is it, what's wrong, baby?"

He grabs her to hug and kiss her at the same time. "It's over, baby. Ryan has the embezzler. We can really go on with our lives."

"Are you serious? Did he tell you it was Amber or Lisa?"

"He didn't say which one. I know it's one of them, though. Baby, what would make a woman do something like that, don't they realize they are destroying other people's lives?"

"Sweetheart, there are so many women who will do anything to get a man and when the man rejects them, they will do anything for revenge. There are a lot of women who think a man completes them and they have got to have a man in their lives to feel whole. They are the ones who are not thinking about the other people they might hurt, because they're hurting themselves. They don't care who might get hurt because of what they want."

"I guess you're right. I am so glad I have a powerful woman in my life who wants me, but does not need me to where she would do anything to get me. I'm just ready for this to be over so we can move forward."

"Thank God. I'm so glad we can put all of this behind us. I am just ready to have a normal life with my man to plan our wedding and get ready for our baby. These last few months have been too much for anyone to deal with. Are you going down to the police station to see who it is?"

Michael goes to their coat closet to get out his trench coat. "Yes, I am waiting for my dad, Uncle Matt, and Uncle Charlie so we can meet Ryan at the police station. They should be here any minute. Don't go to sleep, baby, because I'm going to want to see you when I get back."

Tamara back to herself has a devious smile on her face. "Not only will I be waiting for you, but I will be butt naked, so I can put something on you. You better watch out because I am going to do things to you when you get back that you have only dreamed about. I need to make up for feeling so bad and all the things we have been going through."

"Damn girl, you're going to make me call them and tell them to go without me. Hell, I'd rather stay here with you; they can tell me who was trying to send me to jail." Michael goes over to kiss her and to fondle her breast at the same time as she moans and grabs the front of his pants.

The doorbell rings, and they pull away from each other. Michael goes to let his family in. The dads tell him to come on because they cannot wait to find out who has done this. Michael whispers in Tamara's ear.

"We'll continue this as soon as I get back home."

All four men pace the floor in the area they are told to wait for Ryan and Steve. They are still questioning whoever did this and when they finish, they will bring the person by for them to see on their way to being booked.

"I can't believe another woman has caused this much trouble again." Mike Sr. clasps his hands behind his back.

"Remember, when we found out what Barbara did to James, and I said I was going to come back and fire everyone who wore a skirt in my office. I was just joking, but I guess I should have done it." Michael tilts his head and presses his lips while sitting there with his trench coat still on.

Charlie stands there and looks out the window. "I just do not understand why stuff like this keeps happening to this family. We raised all of you to be fine men and women. The girls like to disappear, and you guys always get some nutcases to work for you. Michael, is that girl still stalking you? I cannot believe some woman is so bold to call your house and hold the phone. What is wrong with all the women you guys surround yourself with? If you do not have crazy women working for you, you have crazy women that you're dating."

"She's pulled back because I'm not getting any more phone calls in the middle of the night with someone just holding the phone. She called when Tamara first came back, and Tamara answered the phone. I'm telling you, I didn't know some of those cuss words even exist."

All the men laugh when Matt Sr. with a twinkle in his eyes. "Bless her heart, she didn't realize she got the wrong one messing with Tamara's man. That girl did not know Tamara and Dianna are crazy. I don't know how crazy Tamara is, but I know for a fact Dianna does not have a lick of sense."

"Trust me. I know my future wife and she's just as crazy as Dianna and you do not want to mess up and have both on your case. You're in a world of trouble."

Mike Sr. looks out the window. "I know this better be the last time we deal with any crazy women at work or personal. You guys need to settle down and hire no more women to work for you, period. We are getting too old for this and I'm tired of the drama."

All they can do now is to wait because they do not know who in the office would do this to Michael. Finally, the door opens and in walks Ryan and Steve with the person in handcuffs who is trying to send him to jail. All four men stand there in complete shock.

Chapter Thirty-Eight

There stands Bruce Newman, law partner, business manager and Michael's friend from law school and undergrad school. All four men sit down at the same time. No one even considered Bruce would do something like this. Bruce drops his head and for the first time, Michael is speechless. Bruce looks at them and then the guard takes him away.

Finally, Michael asks, "Why and how did you know it was him?"

Ryan feels sorry for his friend because it was someone he trusted. "Bruce has a serious cocaine habit, and he needed the money to support his habit. I knew it had to be someone who knew you well and had some power to embezzle money like he was. What made me think it might be him was when I found out Amber had a restraining order against her, but he still hired her. I couldn't figure out why would a law firm hire a lawyer who has a restraining order against them."

Steve jumps into the conversation. "When Ryan told me, we both knew whoever hired her did it for a reason. They wanted to use that for their benefit. When I found out Bruce hired her, and you... didn't even meet her until after he hired her, we knew he kept it from you and everyone else because he had a motive."

Ryan sips on his Starbucks. "He knew her history and knew she would fall for you because all the women do, and he knew that. He set you up Michael because of your lifestyle. Then he planned to set Amber up to be the one who was embezzling. He told us everything once he was caught. She fell for you; she already had a restraining order against her from stalking an attorney she worked with. When it was made clear you were in love with Tamara it made sense, she would do it for revenge."

Steve sits on the edge of the desk. "Once we pinpointed it could be Bruce that's when we subpoenaed his bank accounts and saw he was making big deposits in a new account. We watched his accounts to see how he was living. Your boy Bruce had an entire other life outside the office. He went to wild parties, drugs, and prostitutes. We followed him from work this morning straight to his dealer where we saw him buying drugs. We called the drug enforcers, and they busted him and his dealers. Once we did that, we had him right where we wanted him."

Ryan smiles. "He confesses everything because he knew we had him. What he was doing was increasing the invoices billing hours and generating a check base on that invoice. Prior to running the checks, he would change the vendor's name to his and split into two payments, one legitimate and the other to him. Even though for a minute I thought it could be Lisa, but after checking her out she is clean. Her ex-husband left her in a financial bind and just like any single mother, she wanted to stay in her house and keep her boys in their same school; she just needed some more money to survive. Looking at her life, she does not live out of her means. She just wanted to provide a stable home for her kids."

Mike Sr. steps back. "Ryan, we don't know how to thank you. Again, you save our family."

Michael stands up to embrace him. "Man, we do not know what we would do without you. Thank you for saving my life. I can now get married and have my child without worrying about this situation. I cannot believe quiet Bruce had an entire other life.

I thought all he did was work. He never talked about women or anything else."

Ryan bumps fist with Michael. "You guys need to put me on retainer because I swear you guys have the strangest stuff happening to you. I can't wait for my next case."

Charlie pats him on the back. "We told you there will be no more drama for this family. Everyone is married and with kids, so we will not need your help for anything else. You are more than welcome to attend any family functions, but no more drama."

All the men laugh as they leave the police station. Ryan said he is leaving out tomorrow morning going back to L.A. and promises Michael he will be back in February for his wedding. The dads drop Michael off at home, where Tamara is waiting for him.

She rushes to him as soon as he comes in the door. "You okay, baby? Who was it?"

He tells her everything that happened at the police station, and she is in shock just as much as he is. He tells her he is going to call his boys to let them know what has happened. Tamara tells him she is going upstairs to get ready for bed.

Michael does a conference call to James, Matthew, and Joshua. "Guys, I'm a free man. Ryan caught the person who was embezzling and setting me up to take the fall."

James asks. "What woman in your office was trying to send you to jail?"

"Brace yourself, men... it was not a woman, but a man. Bruce Newman, my law partner and friend, was the one."

Matthew's mouth opened. "You have got to be kidding? Well, at least the curse of women trying to destroy our lives has been broken. Every one of us has had some crazy woman to upset our lives."

Joshua gets into the conversation. "I'm glad since I'm a part of the team. I was nervous of what some woman was going to do to me since you guys seem to have bad luck with women who work for you or are connected to your women."

All the guys laugh until Michael looks up and sees Tamara

standing there completely naked. "Uh...guys, I gotta go because my woman is standing here naked, and I think she wants me."

Joshua hollers into the phone. "TMI... I do not want to hear about my sister in that way, shape, or form. I'm hanging up now."

James and Matthew say at the same time, "I am too."

Michael cracks up laughing, gets up to go over to Tamara to sweep her off her feet. "Baby, they did not want to hear about how you were naked and wanting me. I don't know what's wrong with my boys, we used to be able to talk about anything."

"They're just jealous, baby. Remember when I told you I was going to do things to you, you have dreamed about."

"Yes."

Tamara whispers in his ear what she was going to do.

Michael turns red. "Baby, can we do that all night?"

"We can do it all night long until early in the morning. Mr. St. John, I'm going to rock your world."

Epilogue

Thank goodness Valentine's Day falls on a Saturday the next year because everyone is back in Memphis for Michael and Tamara's wedding. Tamara is five months pregnant and like Dianna, she does not have the strength or energy to deal with a large wedding. They have a small affair at the Peabody Hotel where they have a room set up for them to exchange vows and a room for the reception. Everyone arrives Friday for the wedding dinner except Joshua. As usual, he's tied up with business and would not get in until right before the wedding. Alexandra is there Friday night, and she looks great because she has let her curly hair grow out past her shoulders, which makes her have a natural sexy look. The lady's corner her at the wedding dinner to ask about her and Joshua.

"So, have you two been hanging out in New York?" Dianna presses her lips with a slight frown because she always is the one who gets all in everyone's business.

"I have not seen or heard from Joshua since I left here at Thanksgiving. He has not called me, and I definitely have not called him."

"You mean to tell me my brother has not even picked up the

phone to call to see how you're doing, even if he did not want to ask you out on a date." Tamara shakes her head, crinkles her nose.

"I told you guys. I might not hear from Joshua once we got back in New York."

"Yeah...we know you told us that, but we thought you two would have hooked up for dinner if nothing else." Christina wide-eyed, not believing they really have not seen each other.

All three women are shocked. They just knew they were messing around back in New York and just not telling anyone. Maybe they really do not have any feelings for each other, but they know they do. They both are fighting it.

"Well, he better be here tomorrow because if he misses my wedding, he won't live to be with anyone." Tamara winks at Michael who stands over in a corner talking to Matthew and James before everyone sits down to eat.

There is nothing but great food and wine along with a lot of laughter as everyone enjoys dinner and Tamara and Michael's last night as single people. Just as they finish dessert, James gets everyone's attention to make a toast.

"First, just let me say I am glad I did not make any bets on this one, because I would have lost. You could not have paid me a million dollars to think I would be at a rehearsal dinner for Michael St. John, who swore he would never marry or never settle down with one woman. Now not only is he settling down with one woman, but he's about to become a husband and father... who knew."

They laugh because everyone knows Michael did not believe in marriage or being with one woman when Matthew stands up to make his toast.

"But...he is, and as my brother-in-law and best friend. I am so proud and happy for him. He has found the one woman who he wants to spend the rest of his life with and start a family. To our friends Michael and Tamara. We all wish you the best of luck and we cannot wait to welcome our niece or nephew to join our family. Also, to all our wives, now that everyone is married with children, hopefully you ladies will not disappear, run away, or have any more drama and we all can live happily ever after."

Everyone is having a great time and when it is time to go, Tamara is going to her future in-laws to spend her last night as a single woman. Michael looks pitiful about her not staying with him.

"Baby, why do you have to sleep at my folk's house tonight? I don't want to be without you."

James shakes his head and laughs. "Man, you're sad. You got the rest of your life to sleep with this woman, be a man."

Michael turns around and looks at his friend up and down frowns. "Shut up. You know you were like a lost puppy when Dianna did the same thing, so don't go there with me."

James throws back his head, cannot do nothing but agree. "You know you're right. I had just got her back, and I did not want to let her go even the night before our wedding. Hell, I don't like to be without her right now after almost three years of marriage."

Matthew shakes his head at both. "Not the two biggest players in the world. Who would have thought the both of you would be this whipped over some woman? You both are just sad."

"No, he didn't go there as messed up as he was and still is over my sister." Michael laughs at his brother-in-law. "Face it, guys... who would have thought four years ago, we all would be married, fathers, and this crazy over three women."

They all bump fists with each other because they know Michael is right; those three women have come into their lives and rocked their complete world. All three know they will do anything and go anywhere for their women. Now Michael, who is going to be a father like his two best friends, will have another person, his child, who will have him wrapped around their finger.

Michael grabs Tamara and kisses her goodnight. "Will you call me baby, before you go to sleep?"

She rubs his face and smiles. "Of course, baby, I'll call you before I fall to sleep."

And they say something they have not said to each other in a long time but used to say it all the time to each other when they depart from each other.

"Talk to you when I talk to you. I love you."

"Talk to you when I talk to you, and I love you too."

The next day on February fourteenth at the Peabody Hotel in downtown Memphis, Tamara Walker exchanges wedding vows with Michael St. John, II. She has on a simple off-white Vera Wang gown which has a high waist because she has an expanding stomach and Michael has on one of his favorite designers, a Ralph Lauren Purple label navy blue suit with a light blue shirt and a navy and light blue tie. The wedding is so simple Dianna and James are the only two attendants who stand up with them.

After exchanging vows, they wrote, everyone goes into the next room for the reception. Michael and Tamara stand in line to greet everyone when they see Joshua, and he is not alone. He has brought a beautiful woman who looks like she is a model to his sister's wedding. Tamara is furious, and Michael just shakes his head. As soon as they get out of the receiving line, Tamara goes to find Alexandra who is with Christina and Dianna, and they are already talking to her.

Tamara runs up to her friend. "Alex, I'm so sorry. I had not talked to Joshua, so I did not know he would bring someone. I don't know what's wrong with my brother."

For the first time Alexandra tries to hold back tears, but they fall. She knows her, and Joshua was not a couple, but she cannot believe he brought another woman there, especially after how he interacted with her last year.

"Alex, please don't cry. Joshua is in denial and is plain crazy. Come on, let us get out of here." Christina hates to see her friend hurting like this.

Joshua left the girl sitting at the table by herself while he stood there with his boys. All the women, including his sister, turns and give him a look that if looks could kill, he would have died right there on the spot while they left with Alexandra.

"Oh, shit." James shakes his head at Joshua. "Man, have you lost your damn mind. What the hell made you bring another woman here to your sister's wedding, even though she is fine as hell, but those women are going to kill you?"

Matthew stares him straight in the eyes. "Talk to us man. We know you're not a low-down dog like that, so what's going on."

"I have to go to her, she's crying."

"NO!" All three shouts at the same time.

Michael, his new brother-in-law, drops his head. "First, our dads are going to kill us because they said we could not go into this year with drama, and I'll be damn if you don't start this year off with major drama. Then our wives are going to give us hell for what you have done to their friend. As before, I am going to go get us a couple of bottles of liquor to talk this out, but I'm not getting drunk with you fools because I do not want to miss my wedding night."

They go to the back to grab a table to talk just like they did three years ago at this same hotel with James when he was going through his drama with Dianna.

Joshua freezes and stares with wide eyes. "You guys know I would never hurt Alexandra, but she has been driving me crazy even though I have not seen or heard from her since Thanksgiving. I'm going to be honest. Maria and I have never slept together. She works for me. I know she looks like a model, but she is a stockbroker who is a wiz on Wall Street. I asked her to be my escort because I was trying to prove to myself Alexandra means nothing to me, and I do not have any feelings for her... but it's not working. The look on her face has just broken my heart. Guys, I do not know what to do. I thought all this time I could not stand Alexandra, but after last year I am so confused about her. We made love and I could not stop thinking about her or that one night. I've been running away from her and what happened that night by not calling her or seeing her."

Joshua hunches his shoulders as he continues to talk to his friends. "I thought bringing someone here with me would erase everything I was feeling. I must be honest with you guys. Maria and I have never even thought about messing around with each other. She is like one of the boys, plus she is dating some model I think she is crazy about. I know now, I have messed up big time bringing someone here I'm not even messing with, especially since it has not stopped me one bit from having feelings for Alexandra. Now she might never talk to me again...I don't know what I was thinking by doing this. It's just my feelings for her are so confusing. I just don't want to deal with what I'm feeling for her. I know that's no excuse for what I have done and how I have made her feel."

Michael backs with two bottles of brandy pours their drinks. "Joshua, that's crazy as hell. Did you not think it would not upset the woman after the way you treated her when you were all lovey dovey with her last year? Man, we told you to go on and face your feelings for that woman, but you wouldn't listen and now look at the mess you have caused and if Maria is so cool why is she looking like she wants to kill you as well? You know you should not be playing these games with any woman. I swear all of this is backfiring on your ass and all of us are going to be in trouble for it. You know those women stick together just like we do and when you hurt one you hurt all of them. Now we all will have to pay for your dumb shit."

Matthew the sane one strokes his neck. "Look guys. We all have done some pretty stupid things with our women, not as crazy as this, but now we got to help him get out of this. Joshua, you have got to straighten this out with her, or all our lives are going to be a living hell. I don't know what you can say or do to get Alexandra to forgive you, but you need to think of something."

James looks at his wife, Matthew's wife, and now Michael's new wife coming toward them. "By the looks on their faces, it's going to take a lot to get out of this one. Heads up guys, here they come."

Tamara walks straight to her brother. "Joshua Stephane Walker, have you lost what little sense you have? Who is that bimbo, and why did you bring her here to my wedding and upset my friend? You have pulled some stunts in your days, but this is simply crazy and stupid."

"Tamara, where is she, is she okay?"

Dianna with her hands on her hips. "Hell no, she's not okay. I cannot believe you pulled this stunt. She is out there in the lobby, and you better go out there and make this right."

Christina cocks her head to the side. "Joshua, we're not playing with you, you better go out there and fix this. I know you and Alexandra have never said you were a couple, but you sure treated her like she was your woman. This was very cold to bring another woman to your sister's wedding that you knew she would be attending."

You did not have to tell Joshua twice, he practically ran out there to talk to Alexandra. He is so upset he does not see Matt Sr. and Mike Sr. standing out there talking where they can hear everything Joshua and Alexandra say to each other. All he can see is Alexandra standing there looking out the window.

"Alex, baby, I'm so—"

Before he can finish, she holds up her hand and glares at him with narrow eyes, then drops her hands while she pierces her nails into her palms. "Save it. I do not want to hear it. You don't owe me an explanation just because we slept together that one night and we were together as a couple during the crisis we went through with Tamara and Michael. You are still free to bring anyone anywhere you want to take them. I thought you had changed, but you are still a player who does not care about anyone but themselves. You have played so many games with women, you do not know what is real and what is not. I never want to see or talk to you again."

She reaches up to caress his face for one more time. "Take care of yourself, Joshua."

She walks off and never looks back out of the hotel, and Joshua stands there and stares at her back until he cannot see her anymore. He put his hands in his pocket and drops his head, walking back into the wedding reception as a broken man.

The dads stand there shakes their heads after he walks off

"Oh hell, here we go again."

"Well... it looks like our adopted son needs some help in getting his woman back."

"I knew it was something going on with them. Why couldn't they just get together like normal people?"

"Because these kids do not do anything normal. Now, she's walked off into the sunset and don't want to have anything to do with him. Which means... our work is not done because we have got to get them back together."

"Mike, how are we going to get two people together who both live in New York, and both travel all the time?"

"I don't know yet. I thought getting my son married was going to be our hardest assignment, but this one is probably going to be the hardest. Alexandra is not like our other girls. She is more serious and it's going to be hard to get her to let go of what just happened."

"But you know, we love a challenge. Let's see we have had a traditional May wedding, Christmas wedding and now a Valentine Day wedding."

"Yeah, but we have never had a destination wedding. If they got married, it would have to be in New York since they both are from there and live there."

"The divas would love to plan a wedding in New York City."

"I say a New Year's Eve wedding in New York next year, what do you think?"

"Christmas in New York is my favorite time of the year and to see our adopted son and daughter get married would be the best present we could ever get."

The dads toast to each other as they start on a new journey of getting Joshua and Alexandra married. They love helping their children find their genuine love, even with all the drama they must go through as a family, it is still worth it.

Be sure to check out our other releases:
www.majorkeypublishing.com/novels

To submit a manuscript to be considered, email us at
submissions@majorkeypublishing.com

Be sure to LIKE our Major Key Publishing page on Facebook!

Made in the USA
Monee, IL
23 May 2023

34383052R00136